EMMANUEL BOOK ONE

OUT OF THE SHADOW

JEFF HUTCHISON

WESTBOW
PRESS
A DIVISION OF THOMAS NELSON

WestBow Press books may be ordered through booksellers or by contacting:

WestBow Press
A Division of Thomas Nelson
1663 Liberty Drive
Bloomington, IN 47403
www.westbowpress.com
1-(866) 928-1240

ISBN: 978-1-4497-1456-7 (sc)
ISBN: 978-1-4497-1457-4 (hbk)
ISBN: 978-1-4497-1455-0 (e)

Library of Congress Control Number: 2011924917

Printed in the United States of America

WestBow Press rev. date:3/22/2011

CHAPTER 1

Football practice had been grueling. The Benworth High School football players had expected an easy practice because the first game of the season was scheduled for the following day. Unfortunately for them, the coaching staff decided to work them extra hard. The humidity of western Pennsylvania took its toll and, by the time practice ended, everyone on the team was exhausted.

It was the last Thursday in August and school was starting on Monday, but none of the players were thinking about the first day of school. They were much too excited about the next nights game against Valley Prep to think about school.

It seemed like the entire town of Benworth, a small suburb north of Pittsburgh, was talking about the team's chances. They believed that this could be the year to win a state championship. They had gotten as far as the state semi-finals the previous season before losing a heartbreaking game to the eventual champs. With several starters returning from last year's squad, the expectations were high.

Matthew Peters, a freshman quarterback, knew that he wouldn't be the starter. That position went to David, his older brother, a senior who had started since his sophomore year.

Matthew sighed as he entered the locker room. He spotted Cody Williams, a junior whom he was competing with for the second string job, changing out of his pads. He wasn't sure, but it seemed like Cody looked at him with disdain.

Sam King, the team's head coach, quickly walked through the locker room and said, "Matthew Peters, I'd like a word with you in my office."

A series of friendly jeers from his teammates filled the room, acting as if he were in trouble.

Matthew entered the office, located in the back of the locker room, and quietly sat in a metal chair opposite Coach King's desk, which was more like a table than an actual desk. Matthew was tall for his age with a lanky build, which suited his quarterback position. He stretched his long legs out under the coach's desk as he slouched in the chair. He ran his hands through his straight, sandy brown hair, moving his bangs out of his eyes. His hair stuck to the top of his head, matted down by sweat. He waited patiently while the coach organized some papers on his desk. He knew that he shouldn't be nervous, but he was anyway, and the silence from Coach King wasn't helping.

Matthew looked around the small office. On the wall behind the desk was a bulletin board that was empty except for a season schedule that was posted to it. To his left were a few team photos from previous years in which the Benworth Eagles had won conference championships. On his right, a water cooler with a stack of paper cups.

Matthew looked across the desk at his coach. Sam King was in his early forties, but looked older. He was short and stocky with a dark brown buzz cut. After a minute or two, which seemed much longer to Matthew, Coach King finally looked up and into Matthew's eyes. He felt intimidated by his stare.

"I'm very proud of how hard you've worked in practice. You keep this up and you'll have a good chance of matching your brother's success."

He nodded and said, "Those are big shoes to fill."

"That's true. David is probably the best quarterback in the history of this school. Your brother has a bright future ahead of him. Tomorrow night, there will be scouts from Pitt, Penn State, Syracuse, West Virginia, Ohio State, and Notre Dame in attendance to watch him. Not only does he have a great college career ahead of him, but I think that he has an excellent chance of making it in the NFL someday."

Matthew wasn't sure how to respond, so he remained silent, fiddling with the number six on his jersey.

Coach King continued, "I asked you in here because I wanted to tell you in person what my decision is regarding second string quarterback. Cody is two years older than you and he has more experience, so I'm going to make him number two and you'll be number three."

Matthew lowered his head and replied, "I understand."

"Don't think that this has anything to do with your performance on the practice field. You've done a great job. In fact, you've done such a good job that I'm going to make you the starter on the junior varsity team. This will give you the necessary experience that you will need in the upcoming years."

"I appreciate that, Coach."

"You're not angry?"

"A little disappointed, maybe, but not angry."

"Good. If you don't mind, tell Cody to come in."

"Sure."

Matthew left the office and found Cody, who had just finished changing, by his locker. He was laughing with some of his teammates when Matthew approached. As he got close, Cody gave him a look that wasn't friendly. As hard as Matthew tried to get along with him, Cody always treated him with a condescending attitude.

"Coach wants to see you in his office."

Cody leaned back against his locker with his arms folded. He was a good four inches taller than Matthew and had a broad build. His bright red hair and freckled face made him look childlike, but his glare made Matthew feel uneasy.

"Do you know what it's about?"

"It's good news for you. You've got the backup job. I'll be playing on the JV team."

Cody chuckled and asked, "No hard feelings?"

Matthew wanted to tell him what was really on his mind, that he thinks Cody is a lousy quarterback and doesn't even deserve to be on the team, let alone be placed above him. He didn't think that it was fair that he had to play for the JV team, but he kept remembering what his dad had taught him about being a good sport, so he sucked it up.

"Of course not. You're a junior and I'm a freshman. My time will come." Matthew extended his hand for a handshake. Cody looked down at Matthew's hand but didn't respond right away. Just when Matthew thought that he wouldn't shake his hand, Cody lightly slapped his hand without actually shaking it.

"Cool. It's not like I'll get much playing time anyway." With disgust on his face, he added, "With all the attention your brother is getting, I'll be lucky to see any action at all. It probably won't be until next year that I'll see any real game time."

Cody walked off toward the office, leaving Matthew standing there alone. He took a deep breath and tried to control his anger. He knew that Cody was jealous of David, and that his contempt for him probably stemmed from that. Matthew slowly shook his head and walked back to his locker.

—

John Thomas was one of Matthew's best friends, along with Mark Andrews and Luke James. The four of them had grown up in the same neighborhood and had been friends for as long as any of them could remember. They were all freshmen and excited to start high school.

John saw Matthew walking toward him as he finished changing from his practice uniform into his street clothes. He was a little shorter than Matthew, but very muscular with short dark hair. He played linebacker and was the only one of the four friends with a realistic chance of seeing any playing time on the varsity team.

He watched as Matthew slowly pulled his jersey over his head. He could tell that Matthew wasn't happy and was undecided about whether or not he should say something. After a few seconds of uncomfortable silence, he finally asked, "What did the coach want?"

Matthew shook his head and said nothing. John thought about pressing the issue, but decided against it. He shrugged his shoulders and looked across the locker room.

That was when he first noticed the bruises on Tim Roman's back.

Tim was the team's kicker, who only played football because the soccer program had been discontinued due to budget cuts. The coaching staff was happy to have Tim because he could kick more accurately than anyone else on the team. He regularly made forty yard field goals in practice. Despite that, a lot of the players resented him because he didn't participate in the contact drills that the rest of the team was required to do.

Tim turned around and saw John looking at him. Tim's usually spiked brown hair laid flat on the top of his head, probably caused from wearing his helmet for the last few hours, but his hair was the farthest thing from John's mind. He was curious as to why Tim's back was so bruised.

They stared at each other for a few seconds. Tim slowly nodded at John, who returned the nod. Tim looked very uncomfortable as he turned back around and continued changing clothes.

John turned and said to Matthew, "Hurry up, we'll meet you outside." He left Matthew there and went outside, where Mark and Luke were waiting for them. A couple minutes later, Matthew joined them and they started walking home.

Luke asked, "What did the coach talk to you about?"

Matthew answered, "Cody is going to be David's backup. I'll be third string."

With a stunned look on his face, Mark said, "You can't be serious! You've outplayed him every day since practice began. How can the coach put him ahead of you?"

Luke replied, "You know why. It's because Cody's father is on the school board. It's politics. If Coach makes him third string, he'll never hear the end of it from Cody's dad."

With his head down and looking defeated, Matthew said, "I'm okay with it. It's not like either one of us will play much this year anyway. With all the hoopla surrounding David, we'll be lucky to see any playing time at all."

John heard all that was being said, but didn't pay any attention to it. His mind was on the bruises that he saw on Tim's back. He wondered what had caused them. Bruises were common for high school football players, but Tim wasn't a typical player. As a kicker, he didn't practice the same way the rest of the team did, and you certainly don't get bruises on your back from kicking a football. John couldn't get the troubled look that Tim had on his face out of his mind. He wanted to ask him about it, but wasn't sure how to approach him since they barely knew each other.

John didn't feel like talking and walked a step or two ahead of the other three. He halfway listened to them talk while he thought about whether or not he should say something to Tim. Behind him, his friends' conversation drifted to other topics. They discussed whether or not they would attend the church youth group that night, how good they thought the Steelers would be that year, what the differences between middle school and high school would be, who the prettiest girl in their class was, and a number of things that fourteen year old boys will talk about at any given time. It was no different from any other day when they would walk home from practice, with the exception of John's silence.

As they turned left on to Main Street, Luke gave John a friendly shove to the back of his shoulder and asked, "What's with you today? You haven't said a word since we left the field."

Rather than tell his friends what was really bugging him, John quickly thought up a lie. "I'm just nervous about the game tomorrow. It's not going to be like the middle school games that we played in last year. They're going to be bigger, stronger, and faster. I don't think you guys realize how intense this is going to be."

John saw how the others were looking at him and knew that they didn't buy it. He slowly turned and continued walking home while looking at the ground in front of him.

—

Matthew wondered what was bothering John, but decided that this wasn't the right time to ask. Luke and Mark looked at him with bewildered looks on their faces. He silently mouthed, "Let it go."

At this point, John was about thirty yards ahead of them, so they picked up the pace to catch up. They caught up to him just as they reached the point on their walk home when they would take a short cut through a wooded area that would take them to Forest Street, where they all lived. They could have continued on Main Street for another half mile or so before turning onto Willow Avenue, which led to Forest Street, but by cutting through the woods, they could get home about ten minutes faster. The path through the woods led to a vacant lot adjacent to Matthew's house, a lot often used by the neighborhood kids to play pickup football and whiffleball games throughout the year.

The first hundred yards into the woods, the path was straight with a downward slope. Tall trees loomed over both sides of the trail, providing much needed shade. As the path twisted to the left, it was intercepted by a small creek that was roughly four feet wide. They would always jump across the creek without ever giving it a second thought.

This day would be different. John reached the creek first and leapt across with ease, followed by Mark and Luke, who kept walking. Matthew jumped across last, and when his right foot landed, it came down on the edge of a tree root, which caused it to turn inward. His entire body weight came down upon it as his ankle rolled to the inside. Matthew heard a snapping sound as sharp pain went up his leg. He fell to his right side and screamed. He reached down and grabbed his ankle while he rolled onto his back.

The other three were about thirty feet ahead of him. They turned around when they heard him cry out and saw him writhing on the ground in agony.

Immediately running back to him, Mark shouted, "What happened?"

"I landed wrong and twisted my ankle. I think it's broken. I heard and felt it snap!"

As soon as John reached him, he dropped to his knees beside him and said, "Let me see." He took Matthew's ankle in his hands and applied a small amount of pressure to it.

Matthew screamed out, "That hurts!"

Tears filled his eyes. He didn't want to cry in front of his friends but was having difficulty holding the tears back.

Very calmly, John said, "Okay. We have to get you home. Is your dad home from work yet?"

Matthew grunted, "He should be."

"Good. We'll help you walk and then your dad can take you to the emergency room. Hopefully it's not broken." Even as he said that, he noticed Matthew's ankle already showing discoloration and swelling up like a balloon, giving him no doubt that it was broken. "Luke, get on his other side and help me lift him up."

Luke moved over to Matthew's left side. Matthew put an arm around each of the shoulders. They were about to lift him up when Mark, who was looking up the path, asked, "Who's that?"

They all looked in the direction that Mark was looking. Walking toward them was a man who looked to be in his thirties, with shoulder length, shaggy brown hair and a scruffy beard. He was about six feet tall and relatively thin. He was dressed in blue jeans, white sneakers, and a gray hoodie, which looked out of place on such a hot day.

With a soft voice, the man asked, "What's wrong?"

John answered, "Our friend hurt his ankle. It might be broken."

"Let me take a look." John moved out of the way and the man bent down by Matthew's side. He put his hands around Matthew's ankle, both hands in a cupping position, one on top and the other on the bottom so that his hands were surrounding Matthew's ankle, he lifted his head, looked to the sky, and then closed his eyes.

Luke looked worried as he asked, "What are you doing?"

At first, Matthew wasn't sure if he was comfortable with this total stranger coming up to look at his injured ankle, but as soon as the man knelt next to him, he felt a sense of peace come over him. He didn't know why, but he trusted him. Immediately after the man wrapped his hands around his ankle and looked to the sky, Matthew felt a warm sensation go through his skin, all the way down to the bone. Within seconds, the pain was gone.

With a perplexed look on his face, Matthew asked, "What... What did you do?"

Luke chimed in, "What happened? What are you talking about?"

Matthew looked at Luke. "The pain is gone."

Now Mark was confused. "What do you mean?"

"Just like I said. The pain is gone." Looking back at the man, Matthew asked, "What did you do?"

The man calmly met his gaze and said, "Get up and walk."

Matthew slowly climbed to his feet and took a few small steps. He continued to test it and put more weight on it. "This is amazing! I feel no pain at all." He looked back to the man and asked, "How did you do that?"

The man just smiled. The other three watched with stunned looks on their faces.

Matthew asked, "Who are you?"

"You can call me Emmanuel."

With that, Emmanuel turned around and walked away in the same direction that he had come from. The four friends watched him walk away without saying anything. Emmanuel disappeared around a bend in the path. After a few seconds of silence, Matthew shook his head as though he was coming out of a trance. He started running after Emmanuel, calling out his name.

The other three followed after him. Matthew looked around frantically for the man, but he was nowhere to be found. "Where did he go?"

They were all trying to understand what had just happened. John asked, "Is the pain really gone?"

"Yes. I don't know how, but when he touched my ankle, I felt heat go through and the pain left me. I can't explain it, but it feels great now."

Mark asked, "Who is that guy? Have any of you ever seen him before?"

The others shook their heads and looked up the path to where they had last seen Emmanuel.

CHAPTER 2

Matthew, Mark, Luke and John, still astonished by what they had just witnessed, stood still in the woods for a few minutes. John broke the silence by asking, "Who do you think that guy was?"

Luke scratched his head of reddish brown hair as he responded, "He looks like he could be homeless."

"I don't think so," Mark replied. "He wasn't dirty and didn't stink. His clothes were kind of old looking, but they were clean. I don't think he's from around here. You'd think that we would've seen him before if he was from Benworth."

John thought deeply before asking, "Why was he walking through the woods alone? And why did he go back the same way that he came from? If he was on his way somewhere, wouldn't he have gone on in the same direction? And where did he disappear to? So much of this doesn't make sense."

"This path leads directly to our neighborhood." Luke added, "The way he came and went back would mean that he came from our area. Maybe he's new in town and was just taking a walk or something."

John thought about this, then shook his head. "You know how our neighbors love to gossip. If someone new moved in, we would've heard about it."

Looking frustrated, Luke asked, "Then who was he? We walk through these woods everyday and never see anyone else, but today, some random guy comes along and fixes Matthew's ankle. Too random for me. There's something about him."

With a perturbed look, Mark asked, "What are you saying? Do you think Emmanuel was here because he knew that Matthew was going to get hurt?"

Luke nodded and shrugged at the same time. "I think it's possible."

"Come on! He's not God!"

Matthew looked at him quizzically and asked, "How do you know?"

Mark looked surprised, but didn't say anything.

Matthew continued, "I think he's Jesus!"

The other three stared at him without speaking. John tried to process in his mind what Matthew had just said.

"Don't look at me like I have two heads," Matthew said loudly. "How else can you explain this? A few minutes ago, my ankle was broken and I was in the worst pain that I've ever been in. He comes along and heals it by simply touching me. Who else in the world can heal a broken bone with a touch? I'm telling you, that was Jesus Christ!"

Mark took a step back. He leaned his tall, thin frame against a tree a few feet off of the path and said, "You sound like a religious fanatic! Why, after two thousand years, would Jesus return to earth just to heal your ankle, then disappear without a trace? Don't you think that he has more important things to worry about?"

"I don't know why, but I believe that he is Jesus."

Luke looked at Mark and said, "It makes sense. We all saw how much pain Matthew was in. His face was as white as a ghost. Emmanuel definitely healed him. You can't deny that."

Mark, shaking his head, said, "Maybe it wasn't broken."

John responded, "It was broken. Luke and I saw it up close. It was swelling up to about twice the normal size before Emmanuel got there. I don't know how, but he did in fact heal it."

Mark looked at John and Luke. "So the two of you think it was Jesus, too?"

John shrugged. "I don't know what to believe, but after what we just witnessed, you can't rule that possibility out."

Mark put his hands on his head and asked, "Do you know how crazy this sounds?"

"No crazier than what we just saw," Luke replied. "Think about it, Mark. Can you come up with any other explanation?"

"No, but I'm still not sure. You know that no one will ever believe this. We should probably keep this to ourselves. People would think that we're insane if we told anyone."

"Yeah, you're right," John said. "Not a word of this to anyone, especially our parents. Agreed?"

The other three nodded.

"Not a word about what?"

They all turned toward the sound of the voice coming from up the path. Jude Iscoe was walking down the path in their direction, along with his friends Scott Herod and Ethan Saul. All three had reputations for causing trouble throughout the town. They would have been entering their senior year of high school, but none of them had any interest in school, so they had made the decision that summer to drop out.

"I asked you punks a question! What are you planning to keep quiet about?" Jude advanced toward them with Scott and Ethan close behind. Jude hulked over them. He was well over six feet tall and heavy for his height. He had dark, stringy hair that hung past his shoulders. He was dressed as he always was, in a black t-shirt and jeans.

Matthew, Mark and Luke all took a step back, but John stood his ground. John was the strongest of his friends and didn't want to show any fear. Jude walked right up to John and towered over him. Jude was a whole head taller.

John looked up at him and said, "None of your business!"

Jude shoved John backward and asked, "You think you're tough?"

This wasn't the first time that they had problems with Jude and his friends. Jude enjoyed bullying the younger kids in the neighborhood.

John shouted back, "Tougher than you!"

Jude, Scott and Ethan laughed, making John feel embarrassed. Although John was in great shape, he knew that he didn't stand a chance in a fight with the older, bigger and stronger foes he now faced. He knew that he was overmatched, but didn't want to back down in front of his friends.

—

While this was going on, Matthew, Mark and Luke were backing up. Mark, who was the fastest of the group, whispered to Matthew and Luke, "Follow my lead."

Before he could do anything, Jude caught sight of them sneaking away. "Where do you think you're going? Now tell me, what are you planning to keep to yourselves? Tell us, and we'll let you walk away. Don't tell us, and we'll beat it out of you. Either way, you'll tell us."

Matthew asked, "Why do you care?"

"Watch your mouth, punk! Your brother isn't here to protect you. You'll tell us because I told you to tell us! Understand?"

John backed up a few steps to join his friends. He looked over to Jude and said, "We're not telling you anything. You're just a bunch of pot smoking losers!"

Jude shouted an obscenity as he quickly walked toward them.

Mark yelled, "Run!"

Mark darted left, to the side of the path, zigzagging between trees, with Matthew, Luke and John close behind. Jude, Scott and Ethan immediately gave chase.

John, running behind the other three, shouted, "Stick together!"

Matthew agreed with this, knowing that if anyone was on his own, Jude and his friends would focus their chase on that one. By staying together, they would have a much better chance of keeping them at bay.

Fortunately, they knew these woods well, having spent a lot of time playing there over the years. As they were being chased, they frequently changed direction, which kept the distance between them and their foes far enough that they weren't in any significant danger. They could hear Jude shouting curses behind them and yelling out threats.

Mark was leading them back to the path at an area where they would have about a two hundred yard sprint out of the woods, into their neighborhood, where they would feel much safer.

Matthew heard John yell out, "Faster! They're gaining on us!"

Matthew risked a glance behind him to see how close their pursuers were. He saw that Jude had fallen behind and was breathing very heavy, but Ethan and Scott, who were leaner and in better shape, were closing the gap, about fifteen yards behind. His adrenaline kicked in and he increased his speed.

Matthew ran hard, right on the heels of Mark. Despite the situation he found himself in, he couldn't help but wonder what would have happened if Emmanuel hadn't been there to heal him. Jude and his friends certainly wouldn't have had any compassion for the injury and probably would have made it very difficult for them to get home. He prayed silently as he ran, thanking the Lord for the healing and asking for strength to keep running through his fatigue. His ankle felt strong. One would never have guessed that just a few minutes earlier, he had been rolling around on the ground in serious pain.

—

Mark reached the path first and cut to his left with Matthew a step behind. A second later, Luke made the turn onto the path, but his foot came down on some loose rocks, causing him to lose his footing. He slid to the ground right in front of John. On instinct, John reached down and grabbed Luke from behind, under his arms, and hoisted him to his feet. They both stumbled forward a few steps before regaining their balance and continued sprinting.

Scott and Ethan were only a few yards behind. Jude was farther back, screaming to his friends to catch up and hold them until he got there.

They all finally reached the end of the woods, coming out into the vacant lot. They ran through the lot and turned right onto Forest Street. Their pursuers were still right behind them, but John could see Matthew's house, a one story, red brick home, a little ways ahead. For the first time since the chase began, he started to feel safe.

—

David Peters was leaning against his father's car in the driveway, talking to his two best friends, Dylan Judge and Hunter Daniels. Dylan was his favorite wide receiver and Hunter was the best running back on the team. It was common for the three of them to spend time together after practice.

They had received a ride home from practice from Donavan Ward, a fellow senior, who played on the offensive line.

Dylan stood about six feet, five inches tall and kept his blond hair cut short. He had great hands and rarely dropped a pass thrown in his direction. David was hoping that they would attend the same college so that they could continue playing ball together.

Hunter was one of the few black players on the team. His body looked like it was sculpted by an artist. Lean, but muscular, without an ounce of fat.

The three of them were all outstanding athletes and the main reason why people in the town believed that they could win a state title.

As they stood in the driveway discussing weekend plans, David's attention was diverted when he saw his younger brother, Matthew, along with his friends, running toward him. A closer look revealed that they were being chased. He looked at his friends and said, "Come on," waving them into the street.

When Ethan and Scott saw David, Dylan and Hunter, they stopped in their tracks. Jude came running up behind and joined his friends. David walked in Jude's direction, flanked on each side by Dylan and Hunter. He asked, "What's this about?"

While huffing and puffing, Jude replied, "You might want to ask your little brother what he was doing in the woods."

Matthew cried out, "We weren't doing anything! We were just walking home from practice."

David glared at Jude. He couldn't believe that Jude was the same person that he was so close to years ago.

David and Jude first met each other in first grade and quickly became best friends. As the years went on, their friendship strengthened. Jude lived with his mother about two blocks away. His parents divorced when he was still a baby. Jude grew up not knowing who his father was.

Their friendship began to go astray when David started playing sports. He was a great athlete and excelled at every sport he played. At first, Jude played on the teams with him, but he could never match David's athleticism. David was always the best player on the team, while Jude spent a lot of time on the bench. When he did play, he didn't play well. Jealousy crept in, and Jude resented David's athletic skills. After a couple years, Jude's frustration caused him to quit playing sports. David tried to encourage him and offered to help, but Jude considered this an insult and walked away from the friendship.

In the ensuing years, David continued his dominance in football, basketball and baseball, while Jude started to get in trouble at school. His grades plummeted. It seemed like he spent more time in the principal's office than he did in class. He took up smoking when he was only thirteen, which led him to try marijuana a year later. He and his friends were also suspected in a series of home invasions over the last year, but nothing could be proven, so charges were never filed.

Jude met David's stare. "These runts are up to something. I overheard them saying that they wouldn't tell anyone. When I asked them what they were talking about, they got smart with me." Pointing a finger at Matthew, he added, "He even spit at me!"

Matthew shouted, "That's a lie!"

David just shook his head while looking at Jude. "I don't believe a word that you say. You have no credibility with me."

Hunter stepped in front of David and asked, "Why don't you just turn around and go home? Whatever happened is over now."

Jude responded by yelling out a racial slur.

Before Hunter could react, David and Dylan grabbed him from behind, preventing him from going after Jude. "I'm cool. I'm cool," Hunter said, reassuring his friends that he wouldn't do anything.

When he was sure that Hunter wouldn't go after Jude, David let him go and took a few steps toward Jude. "Why do you have to bring race into this?"

Jude just smiled coyly and looked at Matthew and his friends standing in the driveway. "This isn't over. We'll be seeing each other again. Next time, you won't have these guys to save your hides."

With that, Jude, Scott and Ethan turned around and headed back to the woods.

CHAPTER 3

The next day, Matthew woke up earlier than usual. The butterflies in his stomach were worse than he'd ever felt before. He tried to convince himself that he had nothing to be nervous about since he most likely wouldn't play, but that only seemed to make it worse.

He went to the kitchen and made himself a bowl of cereal, then went to the dining room table where he joined David, who was eating his own breakfast, four pieces of toast with a glass of orange juice. He also had several vitamins sitting on a napkin that he would take before the morning was over. The stereo was playing the latest tobyMac CD.

Matthew asked, "Are you nervous?"

"Not so much now, but I'm sure that I will be the closer we get to game time."

"I don't understand why, but I'm more nervous now than I've ever been. Why am I so scared when I probably won't even play?"

"It's natural to have jitters before a game. If you don't, there's something wrong with you."

"Do you stay nervous the whole game?"

"No. Once I throw my first pass, I'm fine. I'll get nervous again late in the game if it's close."

Matthew accepted this and went on eating. David took the remainder of his vitamins and said, "Meet me in the backyard when you're done."

Matthew finished, put his shoes on, and went out the back door into the yard, a rectangular lawn enclosed by a chain link fence. David was there doing some stretches. Matthew watched him for a few seconds, admiring his physique. He was frequently told that he looks like his brother, which he took as a compliment. He really looked up to his brother.

It seemed like everything David did, he did well. Matthew knew that a lot of it was natural ability, but he also worked hard during practice and gave a hundred percent every time. David's work ethic inspired Matthew to strive harder in everything he did as well.

Although he wasn't resentful of it, he felt like he was living in David's shadow. A lot of the older kids in the area didn't even know his name. He was often referred to as David's brother or David Junior. He knew that in the upcoming years, he would have to surpass David's accomplishments if he was going to establish his own identity.

Matthew joined David and, for the next hour, they went through a series of light exercises to loosen up, but nothing strenuous. They didn't want to be tired for the game.

When they finished, David locked himself in his bedroom. Matthew knew from experience that David wouldn't come out until it was time to leave for the game. Matthew sometimes wondered what David was doing in there before games. He assumed that he was getting himself mentally prepared, but he didn't know specifically what that entailed.

As the day wore on, Matthew kept thinking about the previous day's events. He wanted to tell David what happened, but was worried that he wouldn't believe him. When he thought about it, he was overwhelmed. If Emmanuel really was Jesus, that meant that he and his friends were the first people in two thousand years to see him. It was too much for him. Doubt crept in. He didn't feel worthy to be visited by Jesus Christ. He tried coming up with other explanations as to how he was healed, but couldn't come up with anything.

He tried doing other things to get his mind off of it. Reading a book didn't help, as his mind kept drifting back to Emmanuel. Playing video games didn't help either. He was too distracted to concentrate. He rode his bike around the block a few times, hoping to see his friends outside, but they were nowhere to be found. He finally settled for watching television, but wasn't really paying attention to the show.

After what seemed like an eternity, it was time to leave for the game. This was an away game, so the team was meeting at the practice field, where they would board a bus that would take them to Valley Prep, their opponents for their first game.

Mark, Luke and John stopped by Matthew and David's house to walk to the field together. David had a driver's license, but didn't have a car of his own, so they would have to walk. Sometimes they would get a ride from one of the parents, but this was not one of those days. Dylan and

Hunter also joined them. They agreed that it would be best if David, Dylan and Hunter went with them in case Jude and his friends were in the area. Matthew was relieved when no one pressed the issue about what happened in the woods the day before. He would much rather not talk about it.

As they took the shortcut through the woods, they passed time by joking around and poking fun at one another. John walked in front of the group, keeping to himself while the others had their laughs.

Matthew on the other hand, was in the rear. He noticed that John was unusually quiet and wondered why. This was the second day in a row that he was acting strange. He made a mental note to ask him about it when he had the chance.

As they walked down the path, he kept looking from side to side. He wasn't sure if he was looking for Emmanuel or Jude. Maybe both. He was dreading the possibility that Jude might be in the woods, even though he had his brother and friends there with him. He would much rather not have to deal with the confrontation.

At the same time, he was hoping to see Emmanuel. He had a lot of questions that he wanted to ask him. He needed to know if he really was Jesus.

He looked ahead and saw Mark and Luke having a great time clowning around with the older kids, whom they looked up to and admired greatly. The way they were acting, one would never have guessed that they had experienced what happened the day before. He shook his head and laughed to himself. He knew that he needed to lighten up. He picked up the pace and caught up with the others. He started having fun with his friends and wished that John would snap out of whatever was bothering him and join in.

When they arrived at the creek, one at a time, they all jumped across. Matthew came up last and hesitated. He looked to the other side, where Luke was looking back at him. Luke gave him a nod, as if to say, *You can do it.*

Matthew nodded back and leapt. He cleared the creek with ease and landed safely. Luke smiled and they both ran ahead to rejoin the group.

A short time later, they arrived at the practice field, across the street from the school. They all went into the locker room, grabbed their equipment and uniforms, and got on the bus. David, Dylan and Hunter went straight to the back of the bus and joined some of the other seniors from the team who were already there. Mark and Luke found a seat about halfway back. Matthew and John sat in the seat directly in front of them.

A couple minutes later, Tim stepped onto the bus. Matthew noticed that he and John made eye contact and held it for a few seconds before Tim looked away. He sat in the front row, behind the driver. He took another look behind him at John, and when he saw that John was still looking at him, he slowly turned back around and looked into his lap, sitting perfectly still. One of the assistant coaches then boarded the bus and sat next to Tim, where they began a quiet conversation. John continued to watch them with an intrigued look on his face.

When the rest of the team and coaching staff arrived, the bus pulled out of the parking lot and headed to Valley Prep. They had a fifteen mile ride ahead of them, along the banks of the Ohio River.

Matthew decided to use this opportunity to ask John why he wasn't himself lately. He could hear Mark and Luke laughing and carrying on behind him and did his best to ignore them.

He looked at John and asked him, "Why are you being so quiet?"

"I just have something on my mind."

"Like what?"

John shook his head and looked down. "It's probably none of my business. I should stay out of it."

This confused Matthew even more. "Tell me what you're thinking. Maybe I can help."

John took a deep breath. He looked to the front of the bus where Tim was still engaged in his conversation with the assistant coach. He then looked all around. Matthew was pretty sure that he was checking to see if anyone was listening to them before he would talk. Finally, he asked quietly, "What do you know about Tim Roman?"

"Probably the same as you do. He was one of the best players on the soccer team before they disbanded the program. He's an only child. His mother was killed in a car accident a few years ago and he lives with his dad. From what I've heard, his dad took his wife's death very hard and started drinking heavily. My dad tells me that he drinks every night over at Floyd's Pub. I know that he's been arrested a few times for starting fights at the bar."

John nodded and said, "Yeah. I've heard all that, too. So, what do you think Tim does at night when his dad is out getting drunk?"

Matthew pondered this for a few seconds before responding, "I don't know. It doesn't seem like it bothers him. He's a nice guy, although kind of shy. People seem to like him. We know that he's smart because he's on the honor roll. Why do you have a sudden interest in him?"

"Yesterday, when we were changing after practice, I noticed that he had bruises all over his back."

"We all have bruises. Football is a rough sport."

"True, but he doesn't practice the same way that we do. He spends most of his time kicking and punting. He never does any of the hitting. Think about it, Matthew. The bruises are on his back, not on his arms and legs like the rest of us."

Matthew sat quietly and tried to think of an explanation, but couldn't.

John continued, "Tim saw me looking at him while he was changing. When he noticed, he looked real uncomfortable. Something about this doesn't sit well with me. I don't want to make any accusations without proof, but I can't help but wonder if his dad is hitting him."

Matthew nodded slowly and thought about the possibility. "Well, we know that his dad likes to drink and fight. Maybe when he comes home at night, he takes his frustrations out on Tim."

"I wish there was a way to find out. It's not like we can walk up to him and ask. If he is being abused, then he needs help."

Luke leaned forward from the seat behind them and asked, "What are you guys so serious about? We're on our way to the first high school game of our lives. Have fun and enjoy it."

Mark chimed in, "Yeah! Have some fun." With that, he playfully swatted Matthew in the back of the head.

Matthew decided to leave the discussion about Tim for another time. He reached back and messed up Mark's curly, shaggy hair. Mark responded by jumping forward and putting Matthew in a headlock.

Coach King looked back from the front of the bus and shouted, "Settle down and act your age!"

Mark sat back down, looked at Luke and said, "I am acting my age." Luke just smiled and chuckled.

For the rest of the ride, they kept the conversation lighthearted and had fun, but Matthew was thinking in the back of his mind about Emmanuel. He sensed that John was thinking about Tim the whole time, since he still wasn't acting like himself.

They arrived at Valley Prep and went into the visiting locker room. Matthew was immediately impressed with what he saw.

Valley Prep was a private school and had the reputation for having some of the richest families in the area send their kids there. The locker rooms had just been built the year before, and everything inside was state of the art.

Matthew looked at David, who seemed to be feeling very loose. He shouted out, "Hey Coach! Why don't we have a locker room like this?"

Coach King responded, "When you get to the NFL and start making millions of dollars, you can pay for it."

David laughed and started changing into his uniform.

When the team had finished changing, the coach led them onto the field to stretch and run through a few plays. They were wearing their away uniforms, which consisted of white jerseys with red numbers, and gray pants. Their helmets were white with a red stripe down the center, and an eagle with outstretched wings emblazoned on each side.

Twenty minutes before the start, the coach brought them back into the locker room to give them some last minute instructions and a pep talk.

All the players sat on benches in front of their lockers, which formed a semi-circle around the room. When Coach King saw that he had everyone's attention, he began speaking. "I'm sure that you've all heard the talk around town this summer. There are big expectations for this team. People are saying that we have a shot at the state championship. Well, they're right. We have an excellent chance. We came close last year. The upperclassmen in this room remember what happened last season. I know that the disappointment of falling short is still painful for me, as it is for you. Let me tell you this. I don't want you thinking about the state championship. I only want you thinking about tonight's game. If you're thinking about anything else besides beating Valley Prep, then your mind is in the wrong place."

Matthew looked over to John, who was watching the coach intently, and wondered if he was as distracted as he was. A lot had happened in the last twenty-four hours. He blinked and tried to clear his head. He looked back at the coach and listened.

"It all starts tonight. I'm proud of how hard you've all worked in practice. Now I want you to take what you've learned and give a hundred percent out there tonight. Losing is not an option. This is the best team that I've ever coached. Now let's take the field and prove that to your opponents and everyone out there."

Coach King turned around and walked toward the entrance to the field. The assistant coaches and most of the players followed.

David, Dylan and Hunter stayed behind. Two seasons earlier, before every game, they got together to pray. The coaching staff knew about it, but chose to look the other way. Some of them, including Coach King, were Christians themselves. They knew that they couldn't be a part of it because Benworth was a public school, so they just pretended that they didn't know about it.

Little by little, the group grew. It mostly consisted of players whose families attended their church. The group had now grown to about twenty players. Matthew stood next to John in the circle and looked across to Mark and Luke on the other side. Matthew was surprised to see Tim join the prayer. He nudged John and motioned toward Tim. A curious look came across his face. Matthew had never seen Tim at church before and wondered whether or not he was a Christian.

Tim stood there with a timid look.

Hunter took the lead as they all held hands. "Father God, we come before You in the name of Jesus. Lord, we thank You for this opportunity tonight. We thank You for the athletic ability that You have given us. We don't ask for victory, we only ask for strength to play our best. We ask for the safety of all the players on both teams, and when the game is over, we want the glory to go to You. We ask all of this in the mighty name of Jesus."

Everybody responded in unison, "Amen!"

They rejoined the rest of the team by the field entrance.

They could hear the public address announcer, "Ladies and gentlemen, please welcome to the field, the Benworth Eagles!"

Coach King yelled out, "Let's go!"

From the bleachers on the visiting side of the field, a roar erupted as the Eagles took the field. There wasn't an empty seat to be found. It appeared as if the whole town had made the trip to see the first game of the season.

Chapter 4

It was game time. David and Hunter, who had been voted captains by the team, walked to midfield for the coin toss. Benworth won and elected to receive.

They returned to the sideline, where David loosened his arm by throwing the ball back and forth with Matthew.

Coach King came over to David and asked, "How are you feeling?"

"I feel good."

"Any nerves?"

"A little, but no worse than normal. I'll be fine."

Coach King cocked his head a little to the side. "I need better than fine. I need great. This is your year, David. Show these scouts that they didn't come out here for nothing."

David just smiled and threw the ball back to Matthew. He held his hand up to signal that he was ready, and walked back to the bench to take a drink of water.

Matthew looked around at his teammates, who were being loud and psyching themselves up. He turned and looked up into the bleachers. He couldn't believe how many people were there. The fans who couldn't find a seat were lined up along the fence that kept the spectators off the field. They were four or five people deep from end zone to end zone. He spotted his parents six rows up in the center. He smiled and nodded to them. He continued looking throughout the bleachers, trying to find people he knew. His eyes were going up and down and back and forth.

His heart jumped! Emmanuel was in the crowd! He was sitting in the top row, all the way to the right side of the stands. He was looking right at Matthew, smiling. Matthew ran over to Luke and Mark and told them, "Emmanuel's here! I just saw him!"

Luke asked, "Where?"

"Top row. All the way to the right."

Luke and Mark both looked to where he was pointing, but Emmanuel wasn't there. Mark said, "I don't see him."

Looking confused, Matthew answered, "He was there. I saw him. Where did he go?"

Luke laughed and said, "You're seeing things." Then he jokingly added, "Maybe it was your head that got injured, not your ankle."

Matthew ignored the gibe and looked around some more, but he couldn't find him. He gave up and turned back toward the field, where the opening kickoff was only seconds away.

—

The Valley Prep Vikings looked sharp as they lined up to kickoff. They sported burgundy jerseys with white numbers. Their last names adorned the backs of their jerseys. The gold colored pants matched their helmets, which had a burgundy V on each side.

Valley Prep's kicker raised his right arm, letting the referee know that he was ready. The ref blew the whistle and the game was underway. The kick was high and long. Hunter caught the ball on the five yard line and started running forward. He cut to the right at the twenty, following a wall of blockers. He turned up field, breaking two tackle attempts before being pushed out of bounds at the Eagles forty-two yard line. The cheering from Benworth's side of the field was loud.

Coach King faced David, putting his hands on his shoulders. "We've got great field position. Now go out there and do your thing." He told him the first play and David jogged onto the field, buckling his chin strap as he went.

There was excitement in the air. A buzz went through the crowd as David lined up behind the center. Hunter stood five yards back as the lone man in the backfield. Dylan was lined up as the wideout to the left.

David took the snap, faked a handoff to Hunter, and took a five step drop. He saw Dylan running a post pattern, two steps ahead of his defender. He threw the pass over the middle, putting the ball right into Dylan's hands, hitting him in stride. Dylan caught the ball and sprinted into the end zone. The Eagles sideline and bleachers were cheering madly.

Valley Prep's side of the field looked stunned.

Tim ran onto the field, kicked the extra point, and Benworth had a 7-0 lead less than a minute into the game.

The already confident Eagles team was even more so now. Shouts of encouragement and high five's filled the sideline.

Across the field, the Vikings demeanor was down. Shoulders were slumped and heads hung low. It appeared as if they had already given up.

Tim led the kicking team onto the field and kicked the ball over everyone's head. The ball landed near the goal line and rolled through the back of the end zone for a touchback. Valley Prep would start their drive at the twenty yard line.

The first two plays were running plays that went for short gains, and the third was a pass attempt that fell incomplete. The Eagles defense was pumped up and looking strong.

Valley Prep punted and the Benworth offense went back on the field.

David led them down the field, completing a few short passes, and Hunter picked up good yardage on a few running plays. They kept the ball in bounds and chewed up a good chunk of time off of the clock.

After a few first downs, the Eagles had a first and goal at the eight yard line. Hunter took the ball from a lateral pitch from David and ran a sweep around the left side, untouched, for an Eagles touchdown. After Tim kicked the extra point, Benworth had a 14-0 lead with about four minutes remaining in the first quarter.

The Eagles defense once again shut down Valley Prep's offense, forcing a punt. The remainder of the first quarter and a good portion of the second were uneventful, with both teams punting the ball back and forth.

Late in the first half, David connected with Dylan for another long gain, inside Valley Prep's five yard line. Two plays later, Hunter scored his second touchdown of the game, giving Benworth a 21-0 lead at halftime.

They returned to the locker room while each schools' respective marching band entertained the crowd.

—

In the visitors' locker room, Coach King rallied the team. He urged them to not let up and keep playing hard. He went over some mistakes the players made, but the overall mood in the room was good.

While the coach was talking, Matthew's mind was drifting to Emmanuel. He was positive that he saw him in the crowd but, just like the day before, he pulled a disappearing act. Why was he doing this? And if he really is Jesus, why would he bother coming to a high school football game? Doesn't he have more important things to worry about? The more he thought about it, the more confused he became. He couldn't understand how Emmanuel, or Jesus, if that's who he really is, would consider him important enough to return to earth just to heal his injury. It was too much for him. His eyes filled with tears. He lowered his head so that none of his teammates would see.

John, sitting next to him, looked over and silently mouthed, "Are you okay?"

Matthew nodded and tried to focus on what the coach was saying.

When the time arrived to return to the field for the second half, he scanned the crowd, looking for Emmanuel, but couldn't find him. A lot of the fans were moving around, talking to one another, or returning from the refreshment stand and restrooms. Disappointment crept in. He really wanted to see Emmanuel.

As the game went on, Matthew became less interested in what was happening on the field, and kept searching the bleachers, hoping to see Emmanuel.

Matthew never got a chance to play, but he wasn't upset about it. He knew going into the game that he probably wouldn't play. With all the scouts there to watch David, he knew that Coach King would keep David in the game for as long as possible.

—

Valley Prep was no match for Benworth. By the end of the third quarter, David had thrown two more touchdown passes and the Eagles led 35-0.

In the fourth quarter, Coach King started substituting players, allowing for some of the underclassmen to play. John was inserted at linebacker, and played well. He made two solo tackles and almost intercepted a slant pass. Luke and Mark played a little on offense, Luke at tight end and Mark at running back. Luke caught a pass for a first down and Mark had three carries for eleven yards.

About halfway through the fourth quarter, David threw another touchdown pass and the Eagles lead increased to 42-0. When he returned to the sidelines, Coach King called him over and said, "Congratulations, Kid! You've just tied a school record for the most touchdown passes in a single game!"

David just smiled and thanked him.

With less than two minutes remaining in the game, Valley Prep held the ball on their own ten yard line. The quarterback took the snap and lost his grip. The ball fell to the ground and an Eagles player pounced on it.

Coach King ran over to David, who was sitting on the bench. "You can break the record right now. Go back in there and throw one more touchdown pass."

David responded, "Let Cody play. I don't care about the record. There's no reason to run the score up."

Coach gave him a hard stare. "Those scouts are still here. This could be the difference between whether or not you get a scholarship. I want you to go back on the field and score one more touchdown." He then switched his gaze to Dylan, sitting next to David, and said, "You go in, too. Get open and catch the ball."

David looked irritated. "The scholarships will be there, Coach. I have nothing more to prove. I really think that you should let Cody get some playing time."

Coach King looked him in the eye and said, "It's not your decision. I told you to go in there and throw another touchdown pass, and you will do it."

David and Dylan looked at each other and shrugged. It was obvious that neither one of them felt good about scoring another touchdown in a blowout game.

Reluctantly, they jogged out to the huddle, called the play, and went up to the line of scrimmage. David barked out the signals, took the snap, and dropped back to pass. Dylan lost his footing as he was running his route and fell to the ground.

David's primary receiver was out of the play!

He looked around the field for someone else to throw to, but nobody was open. The offensive line was starting to break down. To his right, he saw a defensive lineman get past his blocker and run toward him. David turned to run to his left, and from his blindside, a Valley Prep linebacker hit him low, putting his shoulder pads directly to the side of David's left knee. David's body buckled as he crumbled to the ground. He screamed out in pain!

A hush fell over the Benworth sideline.

Coach King and several others from the coaching staff ran onto the field. They surrounded him while they checked on his injury. You could hear a pin drop in the bleachers.

—

Matthew stood on the sidelines, stunned. He looked to his parents in the crowd, They both had concerned looks on their faces.

Hunter came over to Matthew and put his arm around his shoulder. "Don't worry. He's going to be alright."

Matthew nodded but didn't feel any better.

—

Five minutes later, the coaches and medical personnel who had been called to the field, helped David to his feet. A quiet applause came from the crowd. David couldn't walk on his own. He had a man on each side supporting him. Slowly, one small step at a time, David made his way to the bench. He sat while the volunteers worked on him.

Cody took the field, ran a couple running plays, and the clock ran out. The Eagles had won their first game of the season, but no one felt like celebrating. Everybody was worried about David's injury.

It was decided that David would be taken to the hospital for x-rays.

The rest of the team returned to the locker room, changed clothes, and boarded the bus. One would never have guessed, by the somber mood of the team, that they had just won 42-0.

CHAPTER 5

After the game, Matthew rode the bus back to the school, and then got a ride with Luke's grandfather, who they affectionately called "Pops."

Luke had lived with Pops his whole life. His mother died from complications while giving birth to him, and his father wasn't in his life. He took off when Luke was still an infant and no one was quite sure where he was living. Luke's maternal grandparents took him in and they were the only parents that he ever knew. His grandmother succumbed to brain cancer when he was ten years old. Now, it was just Luke and Pops.

Matthew stayed at Luke's house for a couple hours, while his parents took David to the hospital. They passed the time playing video games on the *Playstation* that Pops had bought Luke for his birthday earlier in the year. Matthew played poorly, due to the fact that he couldn't concentrate on the game. Too much was happening and his mind was swimming.

Luke and Pops lived only two houses away from Matthew's family. It was after midnight when he got the call from his parents that they were home. He said goodbye to Luke and Pops and trotted home. Pops walked out to the front of his driveway and watched Matthew until he went in the front door, just to make sure that he got home safely. Matthew felt a little embarrassed to have Pops watch him all the way home at his age, but knew that it was only because Pops cared. Pops was always looking out for the neighborhood kids.

As he walked into the house, he saw a drab looking David sitting on the sofa with his left leg extended and wrapped heavily around the knee. The home was silent. The TV and stereo had not been turned on. The diagnosis was a torn ACL, and it would require surgery to repair. He wouldn't be able to play football anymore this year, and baseball and basketball were most likely out, as well. Any chance of an athletic scholarship was apparently gone.

David sat with a look of stunned disbelief on his face as he sat and listened to his parents fill Matthew in on the news. It must have been too much for David to handle, because he grabbed his crutches, which were leaning against the side of the sofa, and hobbled to his bedroom and closed the door behind him.

Matthew stayed up another twenty minutes talking to his parents before saying goodnight to them. As he walked past David's bedroom, he could see light penetrating the crack between the bottom of the door and the floor. Knowing that David was still awake, he was tempted to knock and see if he wanted to talk, but then thought better of it. He figured that if it had happened to him, he'd probably want to be left alone. Matthew went to his own bedroom and got into bed. It took some time, but he finally fell asleep.

—

Matthew woke up Saturday morning and stayed in bed for a while, staring at the ceiling. Everything was changing. He thought about the previous night and wondered what the future held for his family.

As he laid there, he had no desire to get up. He knew that the mood in the house wouldn't be good, and he was dreading it. He finally took a deep breath and got to his feet. He went into the bathroom, brushed his teeth and took a long shower. When he finished, he put on a t-shirt and jeans, and quietly walked into the living room.

As he walked past David's bedroom, he noticed that the door was still closed. He continued on to the kitchen, where his parents were sitting at the table.

His father, Phil, was drinking coffee and reading the newspaper. His light brown hair, which was usually slicked back, was sticking up in places because he hadn't showered yet.

His mother, Beth, sitting on the opposite side of the table, had a small, stand up mirror in front of her, which she used to apply her makeup. Her shoulder length blonde hair was a little frizzy due to the humidity, which seemed worse than normal on this day.

Matthew took the empty chair between them and asked, "Has David come out of his room yet?"

His mother answered, "Not yet. He's pretty upset. You know how much he loves playing football, and his career is probably over."

Matthew replied, "What do you mean his career is over? He's having surgery, right? He can come back from this."

His dad joined the conversation. "Well, his high school career is over. An injury like this takes months to recover from, possibly up to a year. No college will give him a scholarship at this point. His grades are good enough to get into any school he wants, so he could try his luck as a walk on, but he has a long road of physical therapy ahead of him. It will be a long time before he's back to full strength, not to mention the psychological toll it's sure to take on him. I think it's time to accept the fact that his football playing days are behind him."

Matthew shook his head. "I know David. He can come back from this. One thing David is not is a quitter. He'll recover, play college ball, win the Heisman Trophy, get drafted by the Steelers and win a bunch of Super Bowls."

His dad chuckled and responded, "I love your optimism, son, and if anyone can do that, it's David. But for now, let's just concentrate on giving him support. He's devastated by all of this and needs all the help that we can muster."

Matthew nodded. "Yeah, I can do that." He thought for a few seconds, then added, "He didn't say anything last night when I came home. Did he say anything to you at the hospital or on the way home?"

His mom answered, "He's very angry at the coach. He didn't even want to go in for that last play. The coach talked him into it, so he could break the record. If the coach hadn't been greedy, he never would have gotten hurt. He is extremely bitter right now, so tread lightly when you talk to him."

"Sure. I'm a little upset with the coach, too. How do you two feel about it?"

His mom shrugged. His dad rubbed his chin while he thought about it. "You know, at first, I felt the same way as David. When he first told us about it, I was livid. The game was out of reach and there was no reason to rub their faces in it. This whole thing could have been avoided. But now that I've had time to cool off, I'm trying to be understanding about it. If it wasn't for the school record being on the line, Coach King never would have put David back in. He just wanted David to have another chance to impress the scouts. In an odd way, he really did have David's best interests at heart. It's real easy for us to second guess his decision after the fact. I'm choosing to forgive him. I think that you should, too. In time, I think David will, also."

Matthew thought about it and nodded. "I guess I don't have much of a choice if I plan to continue playing football for the next few years. Has anyone talked to the coach?"

"He called this morning. He's going to stop by later to talk to David. He feels terrible."

"Yeah. He should." Matthew immediately regretted saying this when his dad shot him a cold stare.

The uncomfortable silence was interrupted by the ringing of the telephone, which Matthew was grateful for. He jumped from his seat, grabbed the phone, and walked into the living room to take the call. It was Mark calling, informing him that he, John and Luke were waiting for him near the vacant lot, which they all referred to as *Millie's*.

Millie was an elderly woman who owned the house closest to the lot. Most people thought that she owned the property, but it was actually part of the street, thus owned by the city. For whatever reason, the name stuck.

Mark told him to bring his bike, so they could go riding on the trails through the woods. This was something that they did often when the weather was nice.

Matthew slipped on his shoes, quietly made his way to the garage, got on his bike and pedaled out of the driveway toward *Millie's*. When he got there, he saw his friends waiting and rode up to them.

John asked how David was. As Matthew filled them in on his condition, all they could do was shake their heads in disbelief. It was difficult for any of them to understand how something like this could happen. David had become somewhat of a legend in Benworth and anything like this happening to him seemed unthinkable.

Matthew decided that he didn't want to talk about it anymore, so he took the lead by jumping back on his bike and headed for the entrance to the trail. The others followed and they quickly forgot about anything else except for the path in front of them. They had a great time racing up and down the trails for the next hour or so. There wasn't even any concern about running into Jude and his friends, because they knew that they could outrun them on their bikes. It was the kind of fun that made any problems go away for the time being.

Matthew, leading the way, took the group up a hill and veered off the path to the left to an area that leveled off, before dropping a long way into a ravine. The other three eagerly followed. This was a spot where they spent a lot of time when they were younger, but hadn't been to for quite some time.

Hanging from a tree branch, about fifteen feet above them, a thick rope dangled. They had always referred to this as *The Tarzan Swing*. They had a lot of fun over the years swinging on this rope. They would grab the rope, get a running start, and swing out over the ravine, back and forth. They often wondered who was responsible for tying the rope to the branch, and how they got up there to do it, since there were no low branches on the tree to climb, but none of them was quite sure. It had always been there since they started coming into these woods, and its origins were a mystery.

They took turns swinging on the rope, laughing and joking as the day went on. After they had their fill on the swing, they walked over to where they had parked their bikes. As they were approaching, they all stopped in their tracks.

Emmanuel was sitting on the ground next to the bikes, his back leaning against a tree.

Matthew took a few steps forward and asked, "Where did you come from?"

"I think that you know the answer to that, Matthew."

"How do you know my name?"

"I think that you know the answer to that, too."

Matthew stood there looking dumbfounded. Emmanuel smiled back at him. The rest of them remained silent, nobody seemed to know what to do or say.

John finally spoke up. "Are you who we think you are?"

Emmanuel rubbed his beard as he responded, "Once again, you already know that answer."

Matthew was losing his patience. "Okay, then, why are you here?"

"I was hoping that I could help you with what you're going through, but I'm sensing a bit of hostility in your voice. Do you want my help?"

Matthew's eyes widened. "Of course. I'm sorry. It's just a bit too much to handle. You showed up out of the blue two days ago, healed me and then disappeared. Then I see you at the game last night, take my eyes off you for five seconds, and you're gone again. I can't help but wonder if you're going to pull another Houdini act on us."

Emmanuel slowly nodded and said, "That's understandable."

Matthew took a seat on the ground in front of him. The others followed suit. "That was you in the crowd last night, wasn't it?"

"Yes, I was there."

"Then, where did you go? I spent most of the game looking all over the bleachers for you and I couldn't find you."

Emmanuel smiled. "I didn't go anywhere. I was there for the whole game."

"So, you know what happened to my brother."

The smile left Emmanuel's face. "Yes. It's very sad."

Mark, who hadn't said anything up to this point, ended his silence. "Forgive my skepticism, but I'm not as convinced as my friends are about who you are. It doesn't make sense to me. If you are who they think you are, why are you bothering to visit us?"

"You're forgiven." Emmanuel smiled once again as he said that. "Let me answer your question with a question. Why wouldn't I come visit you?"

"Because we're just a bunch of kids. Don't you have more important things to deal with?"

"I can understand why you would feel that way, but you need to remember that I love the four of you just as much as I love anyone else. The trials that you go through are just as important to me as the biggest problems in the world."

Mark, with a troubled look on his face, asked, "Is this something that you do often? Appear to people in the woods?"

"No."

"I'm sorry, but this is too much for me to believe." He got up and walked back toward the swing, where he sat back down with his back to the group.

John watched him walk away, then turned back to Emmanuel and asked, "What are you here to help us with?"

"What do you need help with?"

John, looking surprised, said, "A few things, I guess. I could definitely use some advice about something."

Emmanuel asked, "About what?"

"Well, in the locker room the other day, I noticed some bruises on the back of one of our teammates. It didn't look right to me. I'm wondering whether or not he might be being abused by his father."

"Have you asked Tim about it?"

"How did you know it was Tim?"

Emmanuel just shrugged. "It is Tim, isn't it?"

"Yes. Should I talk to him? If my suspicions are wrong, I could really make him mad, and I don't want to start any trouble."

"Get to know him. Become his friend. Once you have his trust, he'll be more likely to open up to you. Don't talk about the bruises. Invite him to do things with you and your friends. Invite him to church. But most of all, just be there for him. He really needs a good friend right now."

"I can do that." John looked back over his shoulder. "What should we do about Mark?"

"Don't do anything. Be patient with him and he'll come around in good time. Some people have more faith than others."

Luke looked confused. "He comes to church with us every week. I don't think there's anything wrong with his faith."

"Well, Luke, just because someone goes to church, it doesn't mean that they have strong faith." Emmanuel lowered his voice a little, probably to make sure that Mark wouldn't be able to hear him. "There are a lot of people in the world who treat church as an obligation. Their hearts aren't in it. They show up to church on Sunday, then go back into the world for the rest of the week. You would never know that they were Christians based on the way that they live their lives. Mark's family falls into that category. I want you guys to encourage him to read his bible more. He's never opened it outside of Sunday school class."

"Wow!" Luke glanced back to where Mark was sitting. "I had no idea. His parents seem like they have it all together."

"They do well financially, but they're having marital problems. Mark's aware of it, too. So are his brother and sister. I want you to promise me that you'll pray for him and his family everyday. Don't ever underestimate how powerful prayer can be."

Luke responded, "I'll pray for them, but there must be more that we could do."

"Just keep praying and be there for him."

Matthew got up and walked over to Emmanuel, extended his hand to him, and said, "Thank you for healing my ankle the other day."

Emmanuel shook his hand firmly and said, "It was my pleasure."

Matthew smiled, took a deep breath, and asked him, "Will you come to my house and heal David's injury?"

Emmanuel sighed, "I would love to, but sometimes my Father allows things like this to happen for a reason."

"What? His entire future is at stake here. He's lost any chance at a scholarship. This injury isn't even his fault. If you healed him, everything would go back to normal. You have to do this for him."

Emmanuel got to his feet, put his hands on Matthew's shoulders, and looked directly into his eyes. "I know that this is difficult for you to understand, but sometimes my Father's will can be confusing. As you get older, you're going to realize that some things that appear bad at the time, turn out to be the best thing in the long run. I want you to trust me on this."

Matthew turned and walked away, saying, "No. There is nothing good about this."

"Trust me, Matthew. I know what I'm talking about."

Matthew turned back around and asked, "Do you love David?"

"Of course. You know that I do."

"Then heal him."

"Matthew, when this is all said and done, a lot more than his knee will be healed."

"The entire team is depending on him."

"I don't want them to depend on him."

Matthew stopped short when he heard that. He still wasn't happy with Emmanuel's decision, but he was starting to understand.

John walked over and put his arm around Matthew's shoulder. They looked at each other and nodded. When they looked back over to Emmanuel, he was gone.

Chapter 6

Upon arriving at home, Matthew learned that Coach King had come for a visit, but David refused to come out of his room. He stayed for about an hour before giving up and leaving.

Dylan and Hunter were still there, hoping David would snap out of it and talk to them. They, too, left without seeing him.

David finally came out of his room long enough to eat dinner, then went back to his room, closing the door behind him. He didn't speak a word to anyone during dinner.

Sunday morning, Matthew woke up and got ready for Sunday school. David refused to go. He told his parents that he didn't want to face the stares and questions that were sure to come his way. He would feel embarrassed by all the sympathy that would come upon him. His mom said that he should go and get used to it, because the same thing would happen the next day at school, and he definitely wasn't staying home and missing the first day. David refused to budge, and his parents finally relented, but made it clear that he would go to school the next day.

Matthew and his parents left for church, leaving David behind. They arrived at Fellowship Trinity, a non-denominational church a few miles from their house. They parked the car in the parking lot near the front doors. Matthew got out of the car and headed to the left, to the adjacent building where they held the high school classes, while his parents fielded questions about David on their way into the sanctuary.

When Matthew walked into the classroom, he was greeted with a barrage of questions about David. There were six other students, including John, and they were all concerned about his condition. He was annoyed by it, but did his best to answer them without showing it.

Zeke Amos, the teacher for the freshman class, sat on a stool in the front of the room. He was in his early twenties, and insisted that the class call him Zeke, not Mr. Amos. Zeke was tall and thin, with shoulder length hair, parted to the side. He was always using his hand to flip his hair out of his eyes.

The classroom consisted of three tables, each eight feet in length, forming a U shape around the room. Matthew took the seat next to John and listened to Zeke tell an amusing story about a bad date that he had gone on the night before. A few more students trickled in, and just as class was ready to start, Luke and Mark came in, laughing about something they had seen in the parking lot.

Zeke asked them if they wanted to share what was so funny with the rest of the class. They shook their heads and kept quiet. They sat next to each other on the opposite side of the room from Matthew and John.

Zeke started the class and told them to open their bibles to the Gospel of Luke, chapter 11. The lesson was on the parable of the friend in need. He explained to the class that the story was meant to encourage people to continue praying, even if it appears that God isn't answering. He gave them the acronym, P.U.S.H., which stands for *Pray Until Something Happens*. Matthew and John exchanged a look. Matthew remembered what Emmanuel had said the day before about praying. He thought that it was ironic that today's lesson was also about prayer.

As Zeke continued teaching the lesson, Matthew kept looking across the room to where Mark and Luke were sitting. Mark didn't seem interested in what Zeke was saying. Every minute or so, he would whisper something to Luke that would make him smile. After a while, it appeared that Luke was getting annoyed by what Mark was telling him.

Matthew also noticed that Mark didn't open his bible. Zeke called on Mark twice during the lesson to answer a question, but both times, Mark just shrugged and declined to give a response.

At the end of class each week, Zeke would take a few minutes to ask the class if they had any prayer requests. Matthew immediately raised his hand and asked the class to pray for David. One student talked about his grandfather, who was having open heart surgery later in the week. Another wanted prayer to help his father quit smoking.

Matthew whispered to John, "Do you want to say anything about Tim?"

John shook his head and whispered back, "I don't want to say anything without proof."

"We don't have to give his name."

"Not yet."

Matthew remembered what Emmanuel had said about praying for Mark's family, but decided to remain quiet, especially with Mark sitting across from him.

Zeke prayed for the requests, then dismissed the class.

John turned to Matthew and asked, "Do you think we should tell Zeke about Emmanuel?"

Matthew looked confused. "I thought you said that we should keep it to ourselves."

"I know, but the more I think about it, the more I wonder whether or not we should tell someone. I trust Zeke."

"I agree that Zeke is a good guy, but what would be the benefit of telling him?"

John scratched his head and appeared deep in thought. "I just feel like we need to tell someone."

Matthew motioned to the other side of the room and said, "Let's see what Mark and Luke think about it."

They walked across the room to where Mark and Luke were poking fun at a drawing that a fellow student had drawn during class and left behind.

John asked, "Hey guys, do you think that we should talk to Zeke about Emmanuel?"

They both turned and looked at him, not sure how to react. Mark finally asked, "Why?"

John answered, "I want to tell someone. Keeping it to myself is driving me crazy."

Mark shook his head. "If you want him to think that you're crazy, go for it."

"Well, I'm going to talk to him. If you guys want to join me, you're welcome." John walked up to the front of the class, where Zeke was putting his books and notes into a book bag. He glanced up and saw John approaching him and nodded to him.

Curiosity got the best of Matthew and he followed John to the front. The others were right behind him. They wanted to know where this conversation would go.

Zeke asked them, "What's going on, guys?"

John, not sure how to start, looked to the floor and said, "This is going to sound crazy, but you have to believe us. We're not making this up."

John proceeded to tell him about meeting Emmanuel in the woods, the healing of Matthew's ankle, that they suspected that he is Jesus Christ, about the second meeting with him and the advice that he gave.

Zeke remained silent throughout the story, nodding a few times. When John finished, he thought for a few seconds, then asked, "Do you really believe that it was Jesus?"

Mark answered, "They do, but I'm not so sure."

Zeke looked at Matthew. "So, this guy healed your broken ankle. How do you know it was broken?"

"Because I heard and felt it break. It was the worst pain that I've ever felt. Within seconds of him touching me, the pain was gone."

Zeke took his glasses off, rubbed his eyes, and put them back on. "Maybe it wasn't hurt as bad as you initially thought."

Matthew turned his attention to John and said, "I knew that we shouldn't have said anything. He doesn't believe any of this."

Zeke, getting defensive, said, "Hold on a minute. I didn't say that I don't believe you. I believe that you met a man in the woods, but I have a hard time believing that he healed you with just a touch, and I definitely don't believe that he's Jesus. Did he tell you that he is Jesus?"

Matthew responded, "We came to that conclusion ourselves. When we asked him, he wouldn't confirm nor deny it."

Zeke nodded. "So, you don't really know for sure."

"No, but it makes sense. I know that my ankle was broken, and now it's healed. Who else could do that?"

"Look. A lot of people have been fooled by charlatans over the years. It could happen to anyone. They are good at tricking people into believing lies. I don't know who this guy is, but there could be dozens of reasons why he's doing this. Maybe he's lonely. Maybe he's looking for attention. Maybe he's planning to start a cult. I don't know, but I want you to promise me that you'll be careful if you see him again. He could be dangerous."

Knowing that it was futile to try to convince him any further, they all agreed and left the classroom to meet their parents in the church sanctuary.

As they walked between the buildings, Mark was acting boastful. "I told you that he's not Jesus. Even Zeke agrees with me."

Matthew, a little upset with how the conversation went, replied, "He's never met him. We have. I know in my heart that Emmanuel and Jesus are one and the same."

"Whatever! If you guys want to believe a lie, go right ahead. I'm not going to fall for it."

The church service had ended a few minutes earlier and Mark walked away from the group to where his parents were standing with his brother and sister. They got into their car and drove off.

The other three went into the sanctuary to find their folks. Matthew used this chance to ask Luke what he and Mark were laughing about when they entered the classroom.

Luke grimaced as he recalled, "There was a girl outside crying. She didn't want to go into class because she's new to the area and doesn't know anyone. We overheard what they were saying. Her parents were giving her a hard time. I don't know why I was laughing. Mark thought that it was funny, but I didn't. I felt sorry for her."

Matthew asked, "Is she a freshman?"

"I think so. She was right outside the door. I guess her parents gave in, since she never came into class. I was hoping that she would come in. She's pretty hot."

Matthew gave him a playful shove and told him that he'd see him at school the next day. He turned to look for his parents and saw them standing in the front of the church, waiting for an opportunity to talk to Pastor Alex.

—

Alex Ezra was the lead pastor of the church. He was close to forty years old, tall with broad shoulders, dark hair and a goatee. He had founded the church about ten years earlier. In the ensuing years, the congregation grew to about one thousand members.

Pastor Alex finished praying with a young couple, then turned to Matthew's parents. "Phil and Beth, how are you?"

"We've been better."

"Yes. How is David?"

Beth's eyes filled with tears. "He's taking this very hard. We're not sure what to do."

"This must be tough for the whole family. Where is David? I'd like to pray with him."

Phil answered, "He opted to stay home. I can't say that I blame him. He feels like the whole world is crashing down on him."

Pastor Alex nodded, then added, "If there's anything I can do to help, let me know."

Beth asked, "Could you come visit him? He could really use some encouragement, and he looks up to you."

"Sure. I'm free Wednesday night. Would 7:00 work for you?"

"That would be perfect."

"Great. In the meantime, I'll be praying for your family."

"Thank you, Pastor."

They turned and headed for the exit. Several people wished them well as they left.

Driving home in silence, they each had their thoughts on David. The radio played, but nobody was listening. Most Sundays, they would leave church and go to a local diner for breakfast but, without David, they chose to skip it this week and eat at home.

When they got home, they found David lying on the sofa, watching a movie.

"Feeling any better?"

Without taking his eyes off of the TV, he shrugged his shoulders. His body language showed that he wasn't.

His dad picked up the remote control and turned the television off. "We talked to Pastor Alex this morning. He's coming over on Wednesday night to talk to you."

David sat up. "I don't want to talk to anyone. I'm fine."

"You're not fine. You need to talk to him."

David sighed. "Call him and cancel. Talking about it isn't going to change anything." He grabbed his crutches, pulled himself up, and went back to his room.

—

Matthew watched him walk away and wondered if his older brother, whom he had idolized his whole life, would ever be the same.

CHAPTER 7

The first day of school had arrived. Matthew anxiously got ready. He would never admit it to his friends, but he was excited to start high school. He knew that he wouldn't be the big man on campus anymore, like he was in middle school, but he felt like he was ready for that.

He joined David at the dining room table for breakfast. They ate in silence for the first few minutes. Matthew thought about asking him if he was looking forward to his senior year, but then decided it would be better not to say anything. Under normal circumstances, it would be a good topic of conversation, but Matthew didn't think that David was looking forward to anything right now, except maybe getting his surgery over with.

The silence was getting to Matthew. He needed to talk about something, so he came up with something safe to say. "Do you think that the upperclassmen will give me a hard time?"

For the first time since Friday night, David smiled. "Some of them probably will. The football players will have your back, but when they're not around, there will undoubtedly be a few guys who will want to act tough. It won't be anything that you can't handle."

"Did anyone mess with you when you were a freshman?"

"A little bit. Two guys held me down while a third took my shoes. I had to go to my next class in my socks. At the end of the period, my shoes were sitting in front of my locker. Another time, someone padlocked my locker. I had to get a janitor to cut the lock with bolt cutters. You'll probably see a few similar things, but it's nothing to worry about."

This was the first time Matthew had heard these stories and couldn't help but laugh out loud. "Did you ever find out who did it?"

"No. Just keep your eyes open. You're one of the more popular kids in your class, so that will make you a target."

The doorbell rang, startling Matthew. David smiled again. "That's Dylan. He's giving me a ride. Do you want to ride with us?"

"No. I'm going to walk with my friends."

"Suit yourself." David grabbed his crutches and went out the front door.

Matthew finished his breakfast and went outside to wait for his friends. While he sat on the porch steps, he felt the nerves creep into his gut. He wasn't sure if he was nervous about the first day of high school, or the JV game after school. Maybe both.

Five minutes later, John and Mark came into view and went up to Luke's door, two houses away. Luke came out and they joined Matthew. They walked down to *Millie's* and into the woods, on their way to the school.

They talked about the JV game. They were all starting at their respective positions and were excited.

Mark was acting arrogant. Matthew wondered if it was irritating Luke and John as much as it was him. The previous year, Mark led the middle school team in rushing and touchdowns. He was now talking about how he would do the same for the JV squad. He had never been one to brag in the past, so this was a surprise to Matthew. What had gotten in to him?

Wanting to change the subject, Matthew blurted out, "I wonder if we'll see Emmanuel this morning."

Mark looked at him and said, "I hope not."

John glared at Mark. "Why do you have a problem with him?"

"Because I think he's a fraud. You guys can believe whatever you want, but I'm not that naïve."

Matthew decided to let it go. He didn't want an argument. He continued to walk without talking, letting the others have their own conversation. He looked around, hoping to see Emmanuel, but he was nowhere to be found. When they reached the creek, he jumped across without giving it a second thought.

—

When they got to school, they went through the front doors. Straight ahead would take them to the gymnasium, to the left the classrooms, and to the right the cafeteria. John looked around, taking in his surroundings. Most of the other students were sitting in the cafeteria, so he went in and found an empty table. His friends followed him to it.

John sat down and looked toward the front doors just as Tim was walking in. John waved his arm to get his attention. Tim saw him and walked over to their table. "What's up?"

John felt a little awkward as he asked, "Do you want to sit down and hang with us?"

Tim looked around for a few seconds, then shrugged his shoulders and said, "Sure."

John wasn't sure what to say. He didn't know Tim very well and only asked him to sit with them because Emmanuel told him to make friends with him. He glanced to the others, trying to get some help. They just stared back. He knew that Tim probably felt uncomfortable sitting with freshman, since he was a junior. John, realizing that he wasn't going to get any help from his friends, needed to come up with something to talk about. He finally uttered, "Do you miss playing soccer?"

"Yeah. I'm still ticked off that they cut the program."

"Well, you're a good kicker. At least you have the football team to play for."

Tim shook his head. "I don't like football. I'm only on the field for kickoffs, field goals and extra points. Punts too, but as good as the offense is, I don't get to do that very often. For me, the whole thing is boring. Kicking a field goal isn't nearly as exciting as scoring a goal on the soccer field."

"Yeah. I guess I can understand that. If they got rid of the football team, I wouldn't be happy playing a different sport."

Tim looked down at his hands, which were resting on the top of the table. "The worst part for me is that I don't think that the other players like me, because all I do is kick. It seems like they look down on me because I don't do any of the hitting."

Matthew joined the conversation. "Why don't you tell the coach that you want to play another position, too? There's no reason why you can't do both?"

"I did. Coach told me that he doesn't want me to risk getting hurt. He said that he wants to make sure I'm healthy in case they need me to kick a field goal late in a close game."

John smiled and said, "Just wait until you kick a game winning field goal. Everyone on the team will want to be your best friend."

Tim smiled back. "If all the games are like last Friday's, I'll never get the chance."

John responded, "Speaking of last Friday, I noticed that you prayed with us. Are you a Christian?"

"My mother was. She used to take me to her church on the other side of town. I haven't gone since she died. My dad doesn't care much for church or religion. He would rather stay at the bar until closing on Saturday night and sleep until early Sunday afternoon."

John's eyebrows went up. "You're always welcome to come to our church with me and my parents. I know they wouldn't mind. We have a great Sunday school program. We wouldn't be in the same class because you're a couple years older, but I know that you'd love it. We also have a great youth group that meets on Thursday nights."

Tim's face lit up. "That would be awesome. I've been wanting to go back to church."

"Cool. Will it be okay with your dad?"

"He'll never know. Like I said, he sleeps until past noon on Sundays. As long as I'm back home again in time to wake him up for the Steelers game, it'll be fine. He won't be happy if he misses the opening kickoff."

John assured him that they would have him home in plenty of time for that, and Tim agreed to go the next Sunday.

The bell rang, signaling the start of class. They all left the cafeteria and headed for first period. Matthew and Luke went to history class, while John and Mark went to algebra.

—

Once they got to class, Matthew and Luke took their seats next to each other. Both of their eyes went to the door as a very pretty girl with long blonde hair walked in. Matthew felt his heart start to beat a little faster. The attraction he felt for her was obvious to anyone who was watching. He couldn't stop staring.

Luke nudged Matthew and said, "That's the girl we saw crying outside the church yesterday!" He must have noticed the look on Matthew's face because he added, "You can stop drooling now."

Matthew gave him a friendly shove and said, "Shut up!"

She went to the teacher and quietly said something to him. He led her to her seat and introduced her to the class. Her name was Kylie Paulson, and she and her family had just moved from upstate New York.

The class began and the teacher passed out textbooks and gave them a summary of what to expect in the upcoming school year. Matthew was barely listening as his attention kept drifting to Kylie. He was hoping for the chance to talk to her between classes.

The class ended and Matthew went to his locker to put his history book away. Two lockers to his left, Kylie was doing the same. His palms started to sweat as he tried to think of something to say to her.

Before he had the chance to say anything, two members of the senior class closed in on him. Matt knew them by their names, Chad and Brock. Chad put himself between Matt and Kylie while Brock went to his other side, pinning him in.

They were both tall and husky, head and shoulders over Matthew. He took one look at them and knew that he was about to get bullied. He attempted to slip away, but Chad placed an open palm against his chest and eased him back beside the locker.

Chad said, "Hey there, David Junior."

"My name's Matthew."

Chad smiled and said, "Whatever, freshman. Have you been introduced to the trash can yet?" He and Brock both grabbed him, Chad around the legs and Brock around his chest. They lifted him off the ground and started carrying him to the big, round trash can against the opposite wall. Matthew squirmed and twisted his body, trying to break free, but the older kids were too strong for him. They got him above the trash can and proceeded to drop him into the can, butt first.

A number of students who witnessed this were laughing. Matthew felt humiliated. He looked over and saw Kylie. She had seen the whole thing. She had a look of pity on her face, but she didn't say anything. After a few seconds, she walked toward her next class.

Matthew wanted to crawl into a hole. He knew that he might face some problems with the upperclassmen, but he couldn't believe that it happened in front of Kylie. There was no way that he could talk to her now. He was too embarrassed.

Mark, who had caught the tail end of what happened as he walked down the hall, came over and helped Matthew out of the trash can. "You want to do something to get even with them?"

"No. It's not worth it."

Mark shook his head and said, "I wouldn't let them get away with it."

Still feeling embarrassed, Matthew replied, "I'm not going to stoop to their level."

"I'll help if you want."

Matthew shook his head. He wanted to forget what had just happened, but he was so mortified by it that he knew it wouldn't leave his memory any time soon.

Seeing that other students were still staring at him, many with condescending smiles on their faces, Matthew wanted to get away as fast as possible. "What class do you have next?"

"Biology."

"Me too. Let's get going."

They headed to biology class, and as they walked in, Matthew saw Kylie sitting in the center of the room. He couldn't believe it. The one person he didn't want to see at that moment, and she was in the class with him. He hoped that she didn't see the scowl on his face when they made eye contact.

Matthew and Mark went to the back of the class and sat down. Mark motioned toward Kylie and said, "I saw that girl crying outside the church yesterday."

"I know. Luke told me."

"I'm going to go introduce myself."

Before Matthew could say anything, Mark walked over to her. He couldn't hear what they were saying, but before long, she was laughing.

Matthew felt jealousy rage through him. Of all the girls in school, he had to talk to Kylie? It bothered him that Mark had such an easy time talking to girls when it made him so nervous. The whole thing infuriated him.

The teacher started the class and Mark returned to his seat. He leaned over to Matthew and whispered, "Is she smoking hot, or what?"

Matthew ignored the comment, too angry to respond.

The next two classes went by quickly, then it was time for lunch. He joined John at the same table they had sat at before classes started. Tim was there too, which seemed to please John. The three enjoyed light conversation while eating.

Matthew looked a few tables across the cafeteria and saw Kylie sitting with some other freshman girls. She was wasting no time making friends.

Mark and Luke entered the cafeteria and Mark made a bee line to Kylie when he saw her. Once again, she was laughing at what he said. After about a minute, Mark walked away and got into the food line. Kylie's eyes followed him the whole way.

Matthew was disgusted. He didn't understand why he was so enamored with a girl he didn't even know. He hadn't even spoken to her, yet he felt his heart longing for her. He'd been attracted to plenty of girls in the past, but none of them had ever had this kind of affect on him.

Looking back over at her, he saw that she was still ogling in Mark's direction. He pushed the remainder of his food away.

John turned to him and asked, "What's wrong?"

"Do you see that blonde girl over there?' John looked to where he was pointing and nodded. Matthew continued, "She was in a couple of my classes this morning. I wanted to talk to her, but things didn't work out the way I'd hoped."

He quickly told the story about what happened with Chad and Brock. John and Tim couldn't hold back their smiles, which irritated Matthew even more.

Tim put his hand on his shoulder and said, "That's a tough break, but don't sweat it. She probably won't even remember it in a few days."

"That's not the worst of it. In my next class, Mark was joking around with her and making her laugh. I think she likes him."

John responded, "It shouldn't take her too long to realize what a goof Mark is. He flirts with every girl in school. Don't let it get to you. If you tell him that you like her, I'm sure that he'll back off."

Just then, Mark and Luke returned from the food line with their trays. They sat down and Mark said, "I met a really hot blonde this morning. I think I might ask her out."

John looked at Matthew with a look that said, *I'm sorry.*

For the rest of the day, he didn't see Kylie. She wasn't in any more of his classes. He found himself looking for her in every class he went to. He was both relieved and disappointed when he didn't see her.

When the school day ended, Matthew went to the football locker room. The varsity squad was getting ready for practice, while the JV team dressed for their game.

He saw Coach King talking to David. He didn't look happy with the coach. He nodded a few times but didn't say much. The coach called Cody over and the three of them went into the office and talked. He could see through the office window, but couldn't hear what they were saying. Matthew was curious about what they were talking about, and assumed that they were giving Cody encouragement, since the role of team leader was new to him.

Upon leaving the office a few minutes later, Coach King said to David, "You're welcome to watch practice."

"I'd rather watch Matthew play in the JV game." Matthew smiled deeply when he heard this.

"Okay, but I think it would help the team a lot if they saw you at practice. They still look up to you. Why don't you stop by once in a while and give the guys some motivation?"

David stared a hole through him. "I'll think about it."

That seemed to satisfy the coach and he walked out to the field.

David hobbled over to Matthew on his crutches and messed up his hair. "Have a great game, little bro."

Matthew felt a rush of excitement run through him. He finished putting on his uniform and ran out to the field to warm up. He saw his parents sitting in the bleachers and gave them a friendly wave and smile.

The game began and Matthew's play was outstanding. His passes were right on target and he even ran the ball himself for several big gains.

Mark also played well, rushing for over one hundred yards and scoring two touchdowns.

In the end, it was a decisive win for the Benworth JV team.

Matthew went home feeling a little better because of the win, but still felt terrible about how the school day went.

—

After dinner, Matthew knocked on David's bedroom door.

"Come in."

Matthew slowly opened the door and cautiously entered. He wasn't sure what kind of mood David was in, so he didn't want to do anything that might set him off.

He was relieved when David cheerfully said, "You looked great in the game today."

"Thanks. I guess it makes up for how my day started."

"What do you mean?"

"First, let me ask you something. How did you and Jocelyn meet?"

Jocelyn was David's girlfriend. They had been dating for the last two years. David shrugged and said, "I've known her since the first grade."

"Sure, but how did you become a couple? How did you ask her out?"

David laughed. "After a basketball game during my sophomore year, me and the guys went to Mario's pizza. She was there with her friends. It started out with small talk. The conversation flowed naturally. Before I left that night, I asked for her number and called her the next day. The next thing I knew, I had a girlfriend. I certainly didn't plan it that way."

"Were you nervous talking to her?"

"Maybe a little. Once I realized that I was falling for her, I already knew that she liked me, too. That made it much easier for me."

Matthew smiled and said, "There's a new girl in school that I like, but I think she likes Mark. He's planning to ask her out."

"Well, there are plenty of cute girls in our school. If she and Mark end up together, you'll just have to set your sights on someone else."

"Mark had no problem just walking up to her and flirting. When I wanted to talk to her, I got so scared. Why don't I have that kind of confidence with girls?"

"We all have a fear of rejection. Some guys handle it better than others. Don't let it bother you. Mark has nothing on you. If this girl doesn't see that, then she's not worth your time."

Matthew smiled and appreciated what his brother said, but it didn't make him feel any better about the situation. He couldn't stop thinking about Kylie. He went to sleep that night and had awful dreams about Mark and Kylie holding hands and kissing.

CHAPTER 8

The next two days were frustrating for Matthew. He couldn't work up the nerve to talk to Kylie and kept getting angry when he would see Mark and her talking and laughing together. He couldn't understand how he could be so confident on the football field, leading the offense as well as he did, and yet have no confidence at all with girls.

Matthew overheard Kylie tell Mark that she thought he played well in the JV game. Matthew didn't even know that she was there. He hoped that she thought the same of how he played, but she never said anything to him. In fact, she rarely looked in his direction.

John, on the other hand, seemed to be doing pretty good, as he and Tim were getting to know each other and becoming friends. Tim was joining them in the cafeteria both in the mornings before class, and at lunch. Matthew was beginning to enjoy his company as well. Luke seemed to like him, but Mark seemed indifferent toward him.

At football practice, Cody began working with the first team offense. A lot of the starters were losing patience with Cody, because his passes weren't nearly as accurate as David's. Cody was also hard on himself when he would make mistakes during practice. More than once, Coach King had to pull him aside to reprimand him about his attitude, explaining to him that he had to be a team leader and act that way. Dylan and Hunter tried to be supportive, but the rest of the starters didn't seem to respect him at all. They felt like their chance for a state championship was gone without David playing quarterback.

David watched the practices from the sidelines, and it was apparent that he hated having to watch. This was supposed to be his season to shine, and it was obviously hard for him to accept the fact that his high school football career was over. If he wanted to be there, he wasn't showing it.

When he agreed to be there to help the team, he made it clear to Coach King that he was doing it for his friends on the team, and not for the coach. His bitterness ran deep.

The one bright spot for David was that he was very helpful with Matthew, urging him on and making sure that he understood what a big difference there was between third string and second. Matthew was excited about the possibility of actually getting some playing time in varsity games.

When practice ended Wednesday afternoon, Matthew joined his friends for their daily walk home. As they walked through the woods, he watched cautiously for Jude and his friends, hoping that they wouldn't see them, and at the same time, hoping that they would see Emmanuel. He was wondering why they hadn't seen him since Saturday. He started to doubt whether or not they would ever see him again.

Mark's arrogant behavior was getting worse. He was bragging to anyone who would listen about his performance in the JV game. Every time Mark talked about Kylie, Matthew would become angry and jealous.

None of them liked the way Mark was acting. They had been friends with him for a long time and didn't like the changes they were seeing in him. When he wasn't around, John would remind the others that Emmanuel had instructed them to pray for him. John told them that the problems Mark was going through at home probably triggered this attitude change. This could be his way of handling it, or maybe it was a cry for help. John kept telling Luke and Matthew to be patient with him and hopefully, it would pass. Matthew agreed, but deep down, he wanted to punch Mark in the mouth.

When Matthew got home, the smell of pork chops filled the house. David was sitting on the sofa, his arm around Jocelyn, the two of them watching TV together. She often joined the family for dinner.

Matthew took a seat on the recliner to watch the show with them. Looking across the room, he envied his brother and the relationship he had with Jocelyn. Her dark hair was long and straight, falling to the middle of her back. Her lengthy legs were draped over the coffee table as she cuddled up with David. Matthew found himself wishing that he could be doing that with Kylie.

Jocelyn, who had grown close to Matthew since she started dating his brother, looked over to him and said, "David tells me that you have a crush on the new girl in school."

Matthew gave David a dirty look, which he responded to by raising his hands, laughing and said, "Sorry, bro."

Jocelyn giggled and said, "Don't worry, Matthew. I won't tell anyone."

Feeling a little embarrassed, Matthew said, "It's fine. It doesn't matter anyway. I think she likes Mark."

"What makes you say that?"

"Well, I see them talking together a lot, and she laughs at almost everything he says. It's obvious that she's interested in him."

Jocelyn pondered this for a few seconds before responding, "Have you talked to her yet?"

"No. I was going to on the first day of school, but before I had the chance, Chad and Brock picked me up and dropped me into a trash can. She saw the whole thing and I have been too humiliated to approach her since."

"Don't worry about it. Mark isn't even in your league. If this girl has any sense at all, she'll see what an idiot Mark is. You'll have your chance."

Matthew blushed. "Thanks. Maybe I'll talk to her tomorrow."

Jocelyn smiled and said, "Attaboy!"

Even as Matthew said this, he knew that he probably wouldn't do it. He had already decided that he wasn't going to pursue her, out of respect for Mark. Even though Mark was acting like a jerk lately, he was still his friend, and he wasn't going to let a girl come between them. He wasn't happy about this decision, but he knew that it was the right one.

Matthew's mother called them to dinner, and they enjoyed a nice meal together. David looked as if he was getting over his anger, as he participated in the conversation and even cracked a few jokes along the way.

When dinner was finished, their parents went to the kitchen to talk, while Matthew, David and Jocelyn returned to the living room and watched *Wheel of Fortune*. They had a good time laughing and competing to see who could solve the puzzle first. Matthew was relieved because he felt like the old David was back.

—

At 7:00, Pastor Alex arrived. David had forgotten that the pastor was visiting and his good mood suddenly vanished.

Jocelyn gave him a quick hug and asked him to call her later. She smiled at Matthew, said goodbye, and left David to talk with the pastor.

Matthew excused himself and went to his bedroom to start on his homework, leaving David and Pastor Alex by themselves. Their parents returned to the kitchen after greeting the pastor.

Alex sat on the recliner that Matthew had previously occupied and looked over to David on the sofa. "So, how are you doing, David?"

"Terrible. What do you expect?"

"Understandable. When is the surgery?"

"Saturday morning at 8:00."

"Very good. I'll be sure to be praying at that time."

David, feeling very irritated, wanted to get up and pace the room, but his injury prevented that. This only made him angrier. "Look. I appreciate your concern, but I really don't feel like talking about it."

"I know you're upset, but sometimes talking about things helps. Tell me what you're angry about."

"Well, I guess I'm mad at the coach more than anything. He's the one who forced me back into the game when I told him I didn't want to go in. If he had listened to me, I never would've gotten hurt."

Alex nodded. "Yeah, I'm sure that's a bitter pill to swallow."

"Now, I've lost any chance at a scholarship."

"You have excellent grades. You'll still be able to go to college."

"I know, but a scholarship would have been nice for my parents. They earn decent money and can afford to send me to school, but I really wanted to take that burden off of them. Then they could enjoy that money for something else. Is there some way to make Coach King pay for my education?"

Pastor Alex laughed. "No. Unfortunately, you can't do that. Do you think that you can find it in your heart to forgive him?"

"I'm sure that I will in time, but right now, I have a lot of bitterness raging inside of me. I feel like my entire career has been snatched from me. I was supposed to get a scholarship. I was supposed to be a star quarterback in college. I was supposed to get drafted into the NFL. I had everything planned out. Now, I have no idea what the future holds for me and I'm scared."

"Well, I can tell you that you have nothing to be afraid of. You're a bright kid and the possibilities are endless. There are so many careers you could choose. What are you planning to major in when you get to college?"

"I still haven't decided. When you think that you have your future all planned out, and then it's taken away, it's difficult to just shift gears and go in a different direction. I need some time to think about what I want to do.

Pastor Alex opened his bible and said, "Jeremiah 29:11 says, 'For I know the plans I have for you,' declares the Lord, 'plans to prosper you and not to harm you. Plans to give you hope and a future.' You see, David, sometimes the Lord has different plans for us than we have for ourselves. What I've learned over the years is that God's plans are always better than our own. It's possible that God doesn't want you to play football anymore. This could be His way of putting you on the path that He has set for you."

David smirked. "That's easy for you to say. You haven't had your dreams crushed like I have."

"That's not true. I'm not sure if you are aware of this, but I was a pretty good athlete in high school, too. I played linebacker and had a fantastic senior season. Just like you, I had scholarship offers. I was planning on signing a letter of intent to attend Pitt, but God had other plans. The last game of the season, I got hurt pretty bad. I was chasing down a running back who was running a sweep. As I was about to make the tackle, I made the mistake of lowering my head. When we made contact, I felt compression in my neck and my whole body went numb. I couldn't move. They took me off the field on a stretcher and the doctors feared that I might be paralyzed from the neck down. Fortunately, it wasn't as bad as they originally thought. In the next couple of days, I regained feeling throughout my body and I eventually made a full recovery. Unfortunately, my football career was over."

"Wow. I had no idea. How did you get over it?"

"I had a lot of support from my family and friends. I won't lie to you. I was mad. I blamed God for what happened. After a while, I came to terms with it and started praying for direction in my life. By the time graduation came around, I had made the decision to go to bible college. Now, I'm a pastor, and I wouldn't trade my life for all the money in the world."

Completely enthralled with what the pastor told him, David asked, "Do you ever wonder what would've happened if you'd never gotten hurt?"

"Quite often, but I know in my heart that I'm happier and more fulfilled with my life as a pastor than I ever could've been as a football star."

David nodded and smiled. "Do you really think that God has plans for me outside of football?"

"I know He does. The fame and fortune that goes along with being a football star is appealing. There's no doubt about that, but take a look at the big stars of our time. Not just sports, but any celebrity. The media is just waiting for these guys to make a mistake so that they can exploit it. Watch the news on any given day and you're sure to see some famous person shielding himself from the paparazzi, because he got caught in some kind of indiscretion. All it takes is one wrong move and your reputation could be tarnished forever. I'm not saying that it would happen to you if you made it to the NFL, but the life of a star is not all it's cracked up to be. I think that it's possible that God is saving you from that life."

"The NFL needs positive role models, too."

"I agree, and I think that you would've made a great one, but you need to trust that God knows what He's doing."

"I haven't given much thought to God since I got hurt. I've been so angry with the coach that it's clouded my vision."

Alex looked deep in thought and asked, "Is that all you're angry about?"

"No. I love playing football and it really hurts knowing that I'll probably never play again."

"People have returned to the field after suffering similar injuries."

"I know, but the doctor is telling me that I have a long road of rehab ahead of me. Any chance of playing college ball will be as a walk on. It's possible, but I need to be realistic about it. It's a weird catch-22. If I go to a big school, I'll most likely be a back up, and if I go to a small school, I'll have a better chance to start, but the exposure won't be there. Either way, my chances of making it to the NFL are slim. The whole thing is so frustrating."

"I think that you're taking your first step in your transition from being a kid to becoming an adult. Later in life, you'll probably look back on this as a positive thing."

David gave the pastor a dark look. "I highly doubt that."

"I know that it's hard to accept, but give it time. When I look back on my neck injury, I know that it was a good thing. I don't know if I was good enough to play pro ball or not, but I do know that my life today is way better than it ever could've been if I had become a football star. I have a beautiful wife and two great kids that I get to spend time with every day. I pastor a church that has a great congregation. I'm healthy and I'm happy. God has blessed me in so many ways that I can't begin to count them. Put your trust in God and He will do the same for you. Psalm 37:4

says 'Delight yourself in the Lord and He will give you the desires of your heart.' I believe that with all of my heart."

David nodded, but was still troubled. "How do I forgive someone that I'm so angry with?"

"Well, that's not an easy question to answer. The anger will probably take some time. I recommend that you pray for him. I've learned from experience that bitterness toward someone goes away when you pray for them. I don't know how or why. It just does."

"I'll give it a try."

"Forgiveness is a choice. Forget about how angry you are and choose to forgive him. It'll amaze you how fast your anger will subside."

When David didn't respond, he added, "Let me ask you something. How often do you read your bible?"

"Almost never. I know that's not the answer you're looking for, but I'm being honest. I love to read, but I prefer fiction. To tell you the truth, I've tried reading the bible before, but I got bored with it."

Pastor Alex looked intently at David. "Would you do something for me?"

"Sure. What is it?"

"I have a bible that I brought with me." Pastor Alex opened the bible to the inside cover as he walked across the room to sit next to David on the sofa. He pointed to the page. "Look here. This has all the dates of the year, with specific passages to read on those days. If you remain faithful to this daily, you will read the entire bible in a year. This is how I got started reading the bible. It only takes twenty to thirty minutes per day. Do you think you could do this?"

David scratched his head. "I guess I could."

"Great. I'm going to give you this bible. It's yours to keep. Try reading it first thing in the morning, even if you have to wake up a little earlier than normal. That's what I do. It's a great way to start your day. If you commit to it and make it a priority, you'll be surprised at how easy it is. You'll probably even start to enjoy it."

"Thank you. I'll do it."

"You're welcome. Well, it's getting late, so I'm going to head home to my family."

David shook his hand and said, "Thanks for coming over. I'll be honest with you. I didn't want you to come. The last thing I wanted to do was talk about this, but now that we have, I'm glad. This helped. I'm still mad about what happened, but I feel a little better about it."

"Just keep praying and read your new bible. Things will get better."

Pastor Alex said his goodbyes and went home.

David did his homework, called Jocelyn like he promised, then went to his room. He picked up a novel he'd been reading, then put it down. He grabbed the bible that the pastor had given him, found the passages that corresponded to that day's date, and quietly read them. When he finished, he set his alarm clock for thirty minutes earlier than usual, preparing to read the bible again the next morning.

He went to sleep that night feeling the best that he'd felt since the injury.

CHAPTER 9

Friday night arrived and it was time for the second game of the season. The game this week was being played at home, so there would be no bus ride.

The Benworth team was going through some warm up drills when the Westfield High School team pulled into the parking lot. They exited their bus and went into the visitor's locker room.

Westfield lost their first game of the season the previous week and weren't expected to have a good team this year. Matthew felt confident that Benworth would beat them even without David playing quarterback.

After the team finished warming up, Coach King called them into the locker room. The team gathered around him for the pre-game pep talk. When he had their full attention, he started. "This team suffered a serious blow last week. Even though we won the game, we lost our starting quarterback." He motioned to David, who was standing off to the side with his crutches. David just stared blankly back at his teammates. Despite his recent conversation with Pastor Alex, he still harbored resentment toward Coach King.

The coach continued, "I've heard that a lot of you feel like we can't win without David. If any of you feel that way, I want you to leave right now. Go watch the game from the bleachers. There is no room on this team for anyone who doesn't believe we can win every game."

Everyone on the team sat still. A few looked around to see if anyone would get up, but nobody did. When the coach was satisfied that nobody wanted to quit, he went on. "Cody Williams is an excellent quarterback, and we have a fantastic team around him. Our defense is second to none."

Matthew perused the room until his eyes locked on Cody and noticed that he looked very nervous. The rest of the team wasn't getting fired up like they did for the first game. It seemed like David's injury had taken the air out of the whole team.

The coach kept talking, but it didn't have the desired effect on the team. The confidence wasn't there.

While the rest of the team went to the locker room exit, waiting for their introduction, Hunter, Dylan and the others stayed behind to pray. Tim joined them for prayer again, which seemed to please John.

When they finished praying, a retching sound was heard from one of the restroom stalls. Mark, who was closest, ran in to see what was going on. He shouted, "Oh great! It's Cody! He's in here puking!"

A chorus of groans came from the rest of the players. They were clearly fed up with the situation. Jay Ashford, a senior lineman, asked, "How are we supposed to win when this guy can't get it together?"

Dylan came to Cody's defense. "Hey! Cut him some slack. We all handle our nerves in different ways. He needs our support right now."

Hunter went to Cody's side and put his arm around his shoulder. "You're alright, aren't you, brother?"

Cody nodded, but his face was as white as a sheet. He didn't look like he was ready to play. Matthew knew that he needed to be ready to play. If Cody couldn't go, and by the looks of things, that was a strong possibility, then he would have to be mentally prepared to step in. He got excited and nervous at the same time.

Coach King returned to the room, asking, "What's going on in here? Cody! Are you ready to play?"

"Yeah. Just a little nervous. That's all."

"Come on, Cody! We're depending on you." He looked around the locker room to the rest of the players. "Let's get with it. It's game time!"

They followed the coach to the exit just as they were being introduced to the crowd. They ran out onto the field. The first thing that Matthew noticed was that the cheering wasn't nearly as loud as it was the previous week. He looked up into the bleachers and saw that the crowd was just as big as the previous week, just not as passionate. It appeared as if the town didn't have as much confidence in the team without David, either.

Matthew wondered if Emmanuel was there. He looked around but couldn't find him. While waiting on the sideline, he and Cody tossed a ball back and forth, keeping their arms loose. Cody seemed reluctant to warm up his freshman backup.

Matthew noticed Mark looking into the stands at Kylie, who was sitting in the first row. Mark waved to her. She smiled and gave an enthusiastic

wave back. The sick feeling returned to Matthew's stomach. He wanted to be happy for his friend, but his jealousy wouldn't allow it.

Benworth won the coin toss and elected to receive. As the special team's players took the field, David pulled Cody aside and gave him some last minute advice. Matthew watched from a distance and wondered what they were talking about. He turned his attention back to the field and tried to clear his head from any distractions. He wanted to be ready if his chance to play occurred.

—

The Westfield Warriors lined up to kickoff, dressed in their road uniforms, white jerseys with green numbers, along with green pants and helmets. A large white W, the team emblem, filled each side of the helmet.

Benworth, in their home duds, red jerseys with white numbers, and gray pants, took the field.   Westfield kicked off and Hunter caught the ball at the five yard line. He returned it to the twenty-four before being gang tackled.

Cody led the offense onto the field and into the huddle to call the first play. The game plan was to have Hunter run the ball as often as possible, only passing when necessary. The first three plays resulted in gains of six, seven, and thirteen yards, bringing the ball to midfield. The offensive line was doing a great job opening holes for Hunter to run through.

The Westfield defense quickly caught on and started stacking the line of scrimmage. The next two plays were stuffed by the defense and the Eagles found themselves with a third and eight.

Coach King reluctantly called a pass play. Dylan ran his pattern to the sideline and was open fifteen yards downfield, but Cody's pass sailed over his head and out of bounds. Benworth was forced to punt.

Tim entered the game and kicked a high spiraling punt. The Westfield receiver called for a fair catch at the eighteen yard line.

The Benworth defense started strong. After two short gains and an incomplete pass, the Warriors punted the ball back to the Eagles.

Westfield again defended the run well, putting eight or nine defenders in the box, not letting Hunter get any significant gains. It was clear that Westfield was going to make Cody beat them with his arm. On another third and long situation, Cody threw the ball over the middle with Dylan as his intended receiver, but the pass was broken up and nearly intercepted. Benworth had to punt again.

As the game went on, the Eagles players and fans were getting flustered with Cody's play. Thankfully, the defense was playing outstanding and keeping Westfield off of the scoreboard. At halftime, the game remained scoreless and Cody had only completed two out of ten pass attempts.

Coach King tried to psych the team up in the locker room, but the confidence of the team was gone. Nobody believed that Cody could lead this team to victory.

—

Matthew couldn't help but wonder if he would be called to step in if Cody continued to play poorly. A part of him wanted Cody to screw up so he could have his chance, but his conscience got the best of him. He knew that his role as the backup included supporting Cody no matter what.

When they returned to the field for the second half, Matthew did his best to rally his teammates on the sideline. He gave words of encouragement to Cody, but was shunned in return.

Some of the players were pumping themselves up, but others seemed to have given up and were just going through the motions.

—

The Eagles defense came out strong to start the second half, forcing Westfield to punt after three plays.

The offense came back out and established a good drive. Hunter managed to pick up a couple first downs, advancing the ball to the Westfield forty yard line. After two short gains, the Eagles found themselves in another passing situation. Dylan lined up in the slot on the right side. He ran his pattern toward the sideline, but Cody's pass was under thrown and a Westfield defensive back was in perfect position for the interception. Dylan chased him downfield and caught him at the ten yard line. Westfield had a first and goal.

Cody returned to the sideline and slammed his helmet to the ground in frustration. Matthew ran over to him to try to calm him down, but he was too upset to be consoled. He looked like he was on the verge of tears.

The defense came up big, preventing the Warriors from scoring a touchdown. On fourth down, the Westfield kicker came out and put them ahead 3-0. It was a moral victory for Benworth, keeping them out of the end zone, but they still trailed. With the offense struggling, things were looking bleak for the Eagles.

The coach decided it was time to make an adjustment. He pulled the offense together on the sideline while they waited for the kickoff. He told them that they would line up in running formations, but use play action. They would try to trick their opponents into thinking that they were running the ball, when it would actually be a pass.

Coach King grabbed Cody by the front of his jersey and said, "I need you to put the ball into Dylan's hands. Can you do that?"

"Yes, Coach. I'm ready."

"Okay. I'm counting on you. If we can pull this off, they'll be off balance the rest of the game."

They returned their attention to the field as Westfield kicked the ball to Hunter. He caught the ball and found a seam up the middle. Thanks to excellent blocking, he returned the ball past midfield and was finally tripped up by a shoestring tackle at the Westfield twenty-eight yard line. The Eagles fans were cheering loud and the sideline had life for the first time all night.

Suddenly, Cody had the support of his teammates. In the huddle, the players were psyching themselves up and encouraging each other. The offense lined up and Cody called out his signals. He took the snap from center, faked the handoff to Hunter, and took a three step drop. The Westfield defense bit on the fake, leaving Dylan all alone running downfield. Cody threw his best pass all night, hitting Dylan right on the numbers for the Benworth touchdown. The Eagles crowd and sideline were going crazy.

Tim kicked the extra point and the Eagles led 7-3.

The Eagles defense continued to play well, keeping Westfield from scoring any more in the third quarter, and well into the fourth, as well. The Benworth offense kept things conservative after taking the lead. Coach King didn't want to take any unnecessary chances in such a close game.

With a little more than three minutes left in the game, Westfield punted from their own forty yard line. The ball was kicked well, flying over Hunter's head and rolling to the Eagles fifteen, where it was downed.

Hunter ran the ball for two short gains, and Westfield called time-out after each play to stop the clock. During the second time-out, Coach King decided to keep things conventional by running the ball again. If they didn't convert the first down, they would force Westfield to use their last remaining time-out. Then they would punt and rely on their defense to hold them for the remainder of the game. The defense was playing so well that the coach was confident that they could keep Westfield out of the end zone.

The play call was for Hunter to run the ball off tackle to the left side. When Cody took the snap, he mistakenly turned to his right. Hunter went to the left, so there was no one there to take the handoff. When Cody realized his error, he panicked. He took a couple steps backward, holding the ball in front of him. A blitzing linebacker came from the side and hit Cody hard, jarring the ball loose. Another Westfield defender happened to be in the perfect spot. He scooped up the ball and raced into the end zone for the Warriors touchdown. The Benworth sideline watched in stunned silence.

The Eagles trailed 10-7 with just over two minutes remaining. Hunter took the ensuing kickoff, but didn't have nearly as much success as the previous one. He was brought down at the Benworth thirty. They had about fifty yards to go to be in Tim's field goal range, which would put the game into overtime, or they had seventy yards to go for the touchdown, which would give them the win.

Cody had one last chance to redeem himself, but on the first pass of the drive, he threw an interception. Westfield ran out the clock and Benworth's record fell to 1-1.

—

The team, dejected and weary, returned to the locker room. Coach King didn't have anything to say, so they changed into their street clothes in silence. Matthew glanced over to Cody's locker and saw that he was crying.

Most of the players were shaking their heads in disbelief. Losing to Westfield was so unlikely that they were too shocked to talk about it.

As Matthew finished changing, Tim came over and asked him and John if they wanted to go to Mario's Pizza. Mario's was a pizzeria in Benworth that was a popular hangout for the high school kids on Friday and Saturday nights. In addition to great food, it also featured a wide selection of popular video games.

Matthew and John agreed to go and, in turn, asked Mark and Luke if they wanted to join them. They were eager to go, so they all met outside the locker room and walked to the restaurant, which was about five blocks from the field.

Mario's was already getting crowded when they walked in. Matthew spotted an empty table near the back and hurried over to claim it. The waitress appeared and they ordered pizza and sodas. Mark and Luke got up to play some video games while they waited for the food to come.

Matthew, John and Tim stayed at the table and talked about a number of things. A great friendship was forming between Tim and John, which made Matthew smile. They were laughing and joking together as though they had been friends for years. Matthew couldn't shake the thought that Tim might be getting abused by his father. If he was, he hid it well. Tim was funny and seemed to be happy.

While laughing at one of Tim's jokes, Matthew observed Mark talking to a cute redhead while she played a video game. He recognized her from school as a girl named Sarah, who was a sophomore. Luke was talking to her friend, Rachel, a blond who was just as pretty as her friend, at the game next to them.

Matthew was a little confused. Why was Mark flirting with Sarah when he was clearly interested in Kylie?

A minute or two later, the waitress brought the food to the table. Mark and Luke returned and brought the girls with them. After quick introductions, they tore into the food. Mark sat very close to Sarah and repeatedly whispered things in her ear, successfully making her laugh each time.

When the food was gone, Sarah and Rachel excused themselves to visit the restroom. "Hurry back," Mark called out while winking at her. She chortled and blushed a little while she and Rachel walked off.

Mark asked the group, "Is she cute, or what?"

Matthew gave him a sideways look and asked, "What about Kylie?"

Mark asked with a shrug, "What about her?"

"I thought you liked her. You said that you were going to ask her out."

"I probably will."

"Then why are you hitting on Sarah?"

"Kylie's not here. What she doesn't know won't hurt her. There's no rule that says I can't date two girls at the same time."

Matthew was becoming furious, but John lightly kicked his shin under the table and gave him a look that said to let it go. Matthew took a deep breath and tried to relax. He went out to get his mind off of the game and have a good time. He wasn't going to let Mark ruin it for him.

The girls returned and sat back down. Mark put his arm around Sarah and chatted with her quietly, ignoring the rest of the table. Luke and Rachel got back up to play more video games.

Matthew was sitting at the table in a spot where he had a good view of the front door. Mark and Sarah were on the other side with their backs to the door.

Kylie walked in with two other freshman girls. Matthew tried to suppress a smile. He knew that Mark had no idea that she was there, and Matthew couldn't wait to see how this would play out.

At first, Kylie didn't see him. The restaurant had gotten even more crowded since their arrival. Kylie and her friends slowly made their way to the back, getting close to where Matthew and his friends were sitting.

She stood frozen for a few seconds when she saw Mark with his arm around Sarah's shoulder. She did not look happy as she nudged her friends and motioned in the direction of Mark. They looked with shocked expressions on their faces. Kylie said something to her friends that Matthew couldn't hear, then walked over to their table.

"Hey Mark, what's up?"

Mark's eyes got huge as he quickly took his arm off of Sarah's shoulder. "Kylie! I didn't know you were here."

"Obviously!"

Mark opened his mouth to say something, but nothing came out. He was busted and didn't know how to handle it. Matthew just watched and smiled.

Kylie stood there with her hands on her hips, waiting to see if Mark would say anything. When he didn't respond, she said, "I guess I'll see you around." She stormed off and rejoined her friends who had gone to the video game area.

Matthew felt a little satisfaction in seeing Mark get humbled, but was still discouraged by the fact that she didn't even acknowledge his presence.

Sarah pushed her chair away from Mark and asked, "What was that about?"

Mark shook his head and said, "That was nothing. She likes me and got jealous. That's all."

Clearly not believing it, Sarah got up and looked down at him. "Then why did you pull your arm away so fast? You know what? I don't need this." She grabbed her purse from the table and marched off.

John and Tim laughed wildly, which made Mark, who was already embarrassed, even angrier. He glared at them, then shifted his attention to Matthew. "Why didn't you tell me that she was here?"

"How could I say anything with Sarah sitting right here? Besides, this was your fault. If you hadn't been greedy and tried to have two girls at once, none of this would've happened."

Mark's face was beet red with rage. After a minute of silence, he leaned back in his chair and tried to regain his cocky swagger that he had earlier in the night. "I'll talk to Kylie later, after she cools off. I'll smooth things out with her."

John looked at Mark and said, "You'd better wait a long time. She looked pretty mad. It'll be a while before she's willing to forgive you." John gave a quick wink to Matthew.

Mark nodded and said, "You're probably right."

Matthew smiled, grasping the fact that John had just bought him time to make his move.

It was getting late, so they paid the bill and called Pops to come give them a ride home.

As they sat on a bench outside the restaurant, waiting for Pops to pick them up, Luke asked, "What happened while I was gone? Sarah came over and literally pulled Rachel away from me. They left without even saying goodbye."

John laughed and filled him in on what he missed. Luke laughed and said to Mark, "Serves you right."

Mark waved his arm and said, "Shut up!" He definitely didn't like them having a laugh at his expense.

Pops pulled up to the curb and they all piled into his minivan. He dropped Tim off first. His house had no lights on.

Pops asked him, "Is your father home?"

"Probably not. He usually goes to the bar on Friday nights."

Pops frowned. "I'm not sure if I like leaving you here by yourself."

"It's okay. I stay by myself all the time."

"You're welcome to stay the night with Luke and myself."

"No, thanks. If I'm not here when my dad comes home, he'll flip out. Thanks for the ride."

Tim ran inside and left Pops with a troubled look on his face.

Matthew thought about telling Pops about his and John's suspicions of abuse, but then decided against it. Pops was already worried about him, and he didn't want to make it worse. Besides, he didn't have any proof. The last thing he wanted to do was falsely accuse someone, especially of something as serious as child abuse.

While they rode the rest of the way home, they made plans for the next day. Matthew suggested that they ride their bikes in the woods again. He was hoping that they would see Emmanuel again, but didn't say so out loud. The others agreed and set the time for noon. Matthew hoped that David would be home from his surgery by then.

Matthew didn't realize how tired he was until he got home. David was already asleep, so he said goodnight to his parents and got into bed. Despite the football team's loss, he felt pretty good. He feel asleep fast, and this time he dreamed that he was the one holding Kylie's hand and kissing her.

CHAPTER 10

Matthew woke up Saturday morning to an empty house. The rest of the family was at the hospital for David's surgery. The phone rang numerous times throughout the morning, most of them from people wanting to know how David was doing. Matthew informed them that David wasn't home yet, but took their names and numbers, promising to get back to them when he had news.

At 10:00, He called his dad on his cell phone to check on David's status. His dad let him know that the surgery was completed, and everything went well. The doctor recommended that David stay in the recovery room for another four hours or so. Matthew returned all the calls that had come in that morning and told them the good news.

Matthew went over to Luke's house and ate lunch with him and Pops. While they waited for Mark and John to get there with their bikes, Pops entertained them by showing them some video tapes of the kids that he had recorded on his camcorder when they were much younger. They shared a lot of laughs as they watched their younger selves act goofy on the TV screen.

At noon, John and Mark showed up and joined them in front of the TV. Within minutes, they were all laughing hysterically. Pops sat in his easy chair and smiled while he watched the kids enjoy themselves. Luke was his only blood relative left, but he loved the rest of the kids as though they were his own grandchildren.

When they finished watching the videotape, they set out to ride their bikes. Just before they left, Pops reminded them to be back by 3:00 to watch the college football game with him. They assured him that they would and proceeded to pedal their bikes out of the driveway, down the street and into the woods.

Just like the prior Saturday, they raced their bikes up and down the trails, having a great time. After about an hour, they decided to cut the ride short and go back to Luke's house to spend some more time with Pops before the game started.

Matthew led the way as they rode back. At the bottom of a small hill, the path cut sharply to the right. Matthew made the turn and suddenly hit his brakes, causing the bike to skid sideways, the tires kicking up dirt and rocks. The other three came to a stop, narrowly avoiding colliding with each other.

Mark shouted out, "Whoa! What are you doing?"

Matthew didn't respond, but instead stared up the path. The rest of them followed his gaze to see what he was looking at.

Emmanuel was walking toward them, dressed in the same gray hoodie and jeans that he wore the other two times they saw him.

When Mark saw who it was, he sarcastically said under his breath, "Oh great!"

Emmanuel smiled and said, "It's nice to see you, too, Mark."

Surprised that he heard him, Mark rolled his eyes and asked, "Why don't you just leave us alone?"

Emmanuel replied, "Because I have some things that I want to talk to you about."

"I'm not interested in anything you have to say."

John got off his bike, stepped between them and faced Mark. "Then don't listen to him. I want to hear what he has to say."

Mark pointed at Emmanuel and said to John, "He is not Jesus. Don't be so gullible." Turning his attention to Emmanuel, he added, "You don't fool me."

Emmanuel looked back at Mark. It appeared to Matthew that his feelings had been hurt by Mark's comments.

Matthew decided to ignore Mark so he could talk to Emmanuel. "David's surgery went well this morning."

Emmanuel nodded and said, "I know."

Mark shot him a disbelieving look, set his bike against a tree, and turned his back to the group. He walked about twenty feet off the side of the path where he took a seat on the ground with his back resting against a tree trunk. He sat there, glaring at Emmanuel with a cold look in his eyes.

Matthew watched this, then turned back to Emmanuel. "He should be coming home any time now. His mood has gotten better the last few days."

Emmanuel put his hand on Matthew's shoulder and said, "He's going to be fine. The talk that he and Pastor Alex had has been very helpful to him."

"How did you know that Pastor Alex talked to him?"

He smiled back and replied, "You'd be surprised if you knew how much I know."

Matthew pushed his hair out of his eyes and asked, "Do you know what they talked about?"

"Of course. Pastor Alex told him to forgive Coach King. He also gave him a bible and instructed him to read it every day. And by the way, that's something that the four of you should be doing, too."

Matthew laughed a little. "I did notice that he has a new bible. I would read mine more often, but I just don't have time."

Emmanuel smiled back at him and said, "Lying is a violation of the ninth commandment. You have plenty of time to read the bible, if you want to. You choose not to."

Feeling embarrassed, Matthew looked away and said, "You're right. I'm sorry."

"You're forgiven."

Wanting to change the subject, Matthew blurted out, "Our football team lost last night."

"I know. I was there."

"Then you saw how poorly Cody played. If David had been able to play, we would have won handily."

"Probably."

Feeling anger start to burn inside of him, Matthew asked, "Then why won't you heal him the way that you healed me?"

Emmanuel put his hands on his shoulders and looked him straight in the eyes. "I explained this to you last week. There is a reason for this that you don't understand, but in time, you will. You have to trust that my Father knows what He's doing."

"This doesn't just affect David and my family. This affects the whole team."

"Like I said, you need to be trusting. I want you to work hard in practice. You need to be ready when your chance to play comes along."

Matthew's eyes widened. "Is the coach going to bench Cody?"

"Just be ready."

Matthew was pleased by this and thought about how cool it would be if he became the starter.

John stepped up and quietly said to Emmanuel, "I'm sorry about the way Mark has been acting. He hasn't been himself, lately."

"Have you been praying for him?"

"Yeah. I've been praying for his whole family, but it doesn't seem to be doing any good."

"Don't be so sure. Keep praying until something happens."

"That's what Zeke said last week."

Emmanuel smiled and gave him a look that told them that he already knew that.

John continued, "I've been spending a lot of time with Tim this week."

"I know you have, and you're doing a great job with him."

"Should I ask him about the bruises?"

"Not yet. Just keep doing what you've been doing. He'll talk to you about it when he's ready."

John looked to the ground as he said, "I feel really bad. He's such a nice guy. When I think about his home life, it makes me angry. His dad is a drunk, his mom is dead, and he's practically raising himself."

"Pray for his father, as well as him. The death of his mother was difficult for both of them. Tim focused on his school work as a way of dealing with it, and his grades are benefiting from that. His father, on the other hand, turned to alcohol. Drinking makes him violent. Pray that his father will recognize that he has a drinking problem and will seek help."

They promised to pray for these things. Matthew got close enough to Emmanuel so that he could talk to him without Mark hearing. "There's a girl at school named Kylie. I like her, but Mark does, too. What should I do about it?"

"Mark may have burned his bridge with her last night." Matthew smiled as he learned that Emmanuel already knew about what happened at Mario's. Emmanuel continued, "The next time you see her, start a conversation with her. Become friends with her first. If that goes well, then you can think about pursuing a romantic relationship with her."

"I don't want a girl to come between me and Mark."

"I have a feeling that Mark won't stay interested in her for much longer."

Matthew smiled and thanked him.

Emmanuel switched his attention to Mark, who was still sitting against the tree. He was staring straight ahead, not paying any mind to Emmanuel.

He called out, "Mark, will you come over here, please?"

Mark looked at him and asked, "Why?"

"I want to show you something."

"If I agree, will you leave me alone?"

"Yes."

He sluggishly got up and took his time walking over to Emmanuel. He looked annoyed as he stopped a couple feet in front of him.

With his left hand, Emmanuel slowly pulled the right sleeve of his hoodie up to his elbow. He showed Mark the top of his wrist, which had an ugly scar about a half inch in diameter. He turned his wrist around so that he could see the matching scar on the other side. He then did the same thing with his left wrist. Mark's jaw dropped as he stood there dumbfounded.

Emmanuel then lifted his hoodie, exposing his stomach. Just below his left ribs was another scar, this one about three inches long. He asked Mark, "Do you want me to take my shoes and socks off, so that you can see my feet?"

Mark shook his head. "No. That won't be necessary."

The others stood there, speechless. Emmanuel put his arms around Mark to give him a hug. Mark's arms remained by his side. He was too stunned to respond. Emmanuel whispered in his ear, "I love you." He then turned to hug the other three, who all eagerly returned the hug. He told them all that he loved them.

Matthew asked him, "When will we see you again?"

"I'll be around. Just keep your eyes open." He turned around and briskly walked around the bend in the path, behind some trees. They could no longer see him.

John looked over to Mark and asked, "Do you believe, now?"

"I'm not sure what I believe."

Luke jumped in and said, "Maybe we should get going. Let's not make Pops watch the game by himself."

They went back to Luke's house and watched the game with Pops. They munched on potato chips and pretzels while they enjoyed the game. Mark was unusually silent during most of the game. Matthew was pretty sure that he was starting to believe that Emmanuel and Jesus were one and the same.

When the game ended, Matthew returned home and was greeted by David and Jocelyn when he entered. David was in a pretty good mood. The doctor was very optimistic about David's chances of making a full recovery. He wouldn't heal in time for basketball season, but baseball in the spring was a realistic possibility. This was the first piece of good news that David had received since his injury, and it had him in good spirits.

It was a good night in the house. Everyone in the family was happy.

When Matthew retired to his room for the night, he took his bible off of the dresser and set it on his bed. He propped his pillows up against the headboard, so he could sit up in bed and read. He thumbed through his bible, thinking about where he should start. He wanted to learn more about Jesus, so he turned to the Gospel of Matthew.

He read the first four chapters and learned about the Lord's birth in Bethlehem and his baptism in the Jordan River by John the Baptist. He was fascinated as he read about Jesus being tempted by the devil. He loved reading about how Jesus called his twelve disciples. When he read about Jesus healing the sick, he felt a connection with those he healed because he was healed in the same way.

He wanted to read more, but his eyes were getting heavy. He decided to read the next three chapters the next day. He was eager to learn about the Sermon on the Mount.

He turned off the light, closed his eyes, and drifted into a peaceful sleep. He couldn't remember a time in his life when he felt better than he did that night.

CHAPTER 11

Matthew arrived at church with his family. As he got out of the car, he saw John and Tim walking through the parking lot together. He flagged them down and they went to the youth center building. They showed Tim where the junior class met, then backtracked to the freshman room.

Matthew and John greeted Zeke and took seats next to each other. A few minutes later, Luke and Mark came in and sat across the room from them.

About five minutes before class started, Kylie walked in. She stopped as she made eye contact with Mark. She looked away quickly, then walked to the opposite side of the room, where she sat next to Matthew. John nudged him from his other side and gave him a big smile.

Kylie set her bible down on the table in front of her, then turned to Matthew and asked, "How are you this morning, Matthew?"

Butterflies stirred up in his stomach. "I'm good." He wanted to say more, but he drew a blank. The fact that she knew his name surprised him. They'd never been formally introduced.

He was flustered with his inability to talk to her without getting nervous. He wished that he could have Mark's confidence with girls.

Kylie took her seat and said, "It's a shame about how the game turned out Friday night."

Without being able to think of anything else to say, he spit out, "Well, you win some and you lose some." He winced after saying it, feeling like a bumbling fool.

She put her hand on his shoulder, which made his heart race. "You know, a lot of people in the crowd were saying that the coach should have put you in the game."

"Really? Who said that?"

"A bunch of people. I don't know who most of them were because I'm new around here, but they were saying it. Nobody was impressed by Cody's play."

"Well. I know that if my brother hadn't gotten hurt last week, we would've won easily."

Kylie smiled at him and said, "And if the coach would've let you play, you would've won easily."

"Do you really think so?"

"I saw you play in the JV game last week. If that's any indication, then I'm sure that you would've played well."

Matthew blushed a little and said, "Thanks. We have another JV game on Tuesday. Are you going to watch?"

"I'll be there. I love football."

"It's an away game. How will you get there?"

She assured him, "I've already talked to some friends. I have a ride."

"Cool. Are you going to watch the Steelers today?"

She shook her head and made a funny face. "I'm not a Steelers fan."

Matthew feigned disbelief and asked her, "Are you aware that that's considered blasphemy around here?"

She laughed and answered, "I'm not from this area. I'm from upstate New York."

"Well then, who's your favorite team? The Bills? The Jets? The Giants?"

"Actually, the Patriots."

Matthew and John said simultaneously, "Oh no!" Kylie laughed a little to herself.

John shouted out, "Hey Zeke! Did you hear that? She's a Patriots fan!"

Zeke laughed and jokingly said, "I'm afraid you're going to have to leave. No Patriots fans are allowed in my class."

Kylie was laughing hard now. "If I convert to the Steelers, my dad will disown me." She was clearly enjoying the attention.

Matthew looked across the room to see Mark's reaction to all of this. He had a small smile, but seemed to be distracted. Luke was laughing with the rest of the class. Matthew hoped that Mark wouldn't be mad at him for joking around with Kylie.

Zeke started the class. The day's lesson was about the Beatitudes. Matthew's ears perked up when he heard this because he knew that the

Beatitudes were the beginning of the Sermon on the Mount. He already had plans to read that later in the day.

Throughout the lesson, Matthew kept looking over to Mark. Just like the previous Sunday, Mark wasn't paying attention. The difference, this week, was that instead of cracking jokes with Luke, he was staring into space.

Zeke noticed this and called on him to answer a question. Mark, upon hearing his name, looked at Zeke and asked, "Huh?"

The class roared with laughter, which normally would have upset him, but he just took it in stride and went back into his trance like state, staring straight ahead. Something was obviously bothering him.

When the class concluded, Kylie turned to Matthew and said, "See you in school."

She started to get up to leave, so Matthew quickly asked, "Would you like to go see a movie with me sometime?"

She sat back down slowly, reached over and softly touched his forearm. "I don't think so. I'm trying to get settled in here. For now, I just want to make friends. You seem like a really nice guy, and maybe someday in the future, I'll take you up on that, but for now, I think that we should keep it as friends."

Matthew was disappointed, but was gracious as he told her, "I understand. I'll see you in class."

Kylie smiled at him, then quietly got up and left the room.

John patted Matthew on the back and said, "Don't let it get you down."

"I won't."

Mark and Luke came across the room. Mark said, "I think we should talk."

John asked, "About what?"

Matthew added, "Yeah. What's wrong? You don't seem yourself today."

Mark took the seat next to John and swiveled sideways to face the rest of them. "I can't stop thinking about what happened in the woods yesterday. I saw Emmanuel's scars up close. I think that I was wrong about him."

Luke asked, "So, what are you trying to say?"

"I'm saying that you guys were right and I was wrong. I hate admitting that, but I now believe that Emmanuel is Jesus."

The other three smiled. John playfully put him in a headlock and messed up his hair. "It's about time that you came around."

While they all laughed, Zeke came over to them. "What's going on?"

"Nothing. Just having a little fun."

Zeke pulled up a chair and asked, "Have you seen that guy in the woods again?"

They all looked at each other but didn't say anything. Zeke nodded and said, "I'll take that as a yes. What did you talk about?"

John answered, "He just gives us advice."

"About what?"

"He tells us to pray."

"That's all?"

"No. there's more, but it doesn't matter. You won't believe us anyway."

Zeke looked down and rubbed his eyes. "You need to be careful with this guy. You have to understand that he isn't who he claims to be."

Matthew responded, "He doesn't claim to be anyone. We figured out who he is on our own."

"What makes you think that he's Jesus?"

"For me, it was when he healed my ankle. Only Jesus could do something like that."

Zeke looked very troubled. "Don't let this guy fool you." Turning his attention to Mark, he added, "You said last week that you didn't believe him. Have you changed your mind?"

Mark nodded. "He showed me his scars. The nail marks on his wrists and where the sword pierced his side."

Zeke gave a disbelieving look. "You're telling me that you saw these scars?"

John said, "We all saw them. He even offered to take his shoes and socks off to show us the scars on his feet, but Mark told him that it wasn't necessary."

"This is really disturbing. Please stay away from him. You have no way of knowing if this guy is dangerous or not."

John responded, "We don't go out looking for him. He just appears from time to time."

"That's even worse. It sounds like this guy is stalking you."

Getting defensive, Matthew retorted, "You don't know him. He's not dangerous. If you met him, you'd understand."

Zeke nodded. "Please be careful with him. Don't tell him anything personal about yourselves. I'm just looking out for your safety."

Feeling frustrated because Zeke didn't believe them, the kids left the room and went home with their families.

—

Zeke got his books and notes together and put them in his car, but instead of leaving, he went into the sanctuary to talk with Pastor Alex. He waited patiently while the pastor talked and prayed with members of the congregation.

When he finished, Zeke approached him. "I have something that I need to talk to you about."

"What is it, Zeke?" The pastor started walking toward the back of the church, where his office was located. Zeke walked by his side.

"I'm worried about some of my students."

"Which ones?"

"John Thomas, Matthew Peters, Luke James and Mark Andrews."

Pastor Alex stopped in his tracks and said, "Those are some pretty bright kids. Not ones that I would expect you to have problems with."

"It's not a discipline problem. It's something else entirely. I'm very troubled by it."

Alex started walking again and said, "Let's talk in my office."

When they got there, Alex sat behind his desk while Zeke sat in one of the two chairs in front. Alex leaned back in his chair and asked, "So, what's bothering you?"

Zeke looked back at him and said, "You're going to find this hard to believe, but those boys are claiming that Jesus has been visiting them."

The pastor's eyes got big. "They told you this? Maybe they were just pulling your leg."

"I don't think so. Apparently, this guy, calling himself Emmanuel, has been coming up to them in the woods and filling their minds with lies. Matthew even said that he broke his ankle and this guy miraculously healed him."

Pastor Alex sat silent for a few seconds before asking, "Has he told them that he's Jesus?"

"They said that he wouldn't confirm nor deny it when they asked him."

"So, aside from this supposed healing, what makes them think that he's Jesus?"

"They also said that he has scars on his wrists and side that match the scars that Jesus had from being crucified."

"We need to find out who this guy is. Do their parents know about this?"

"I don't think so."

Alex scratched his head and took a deep breath. "Thank you for bringing this to my attention. I'm going to call their parents and set up a meeting. You should be there, too. Their parents need to know what's happening."

Zeke agreed to attend the meeting and went home.

—

Alex sat in his office silently, trying to decide the best way to approach this problem. He thought about all the possible motives someone would have to approach teenage boys in the woods, and they all made him shudder. He wanted to address this as fast as he could, before one of the boys got hurt.

Later that night, Pastor Alex made his phone calls and set up a meeting at Pops' house for Tuesday night.

CHAPTER 12

The bus taking the JV team to their game pulled out of the parking lot. Matthew and Mark sat next to each other, engaging in small talk. John and Luke sat in the seat behind them, talking amongst themselves.

After about five minutes, the conversation stalled. Mark said to Matthew, "I noticed that you and Kylie were talking quite a bit on Sunday. Do you like her?"

"I do. I hope it doesn't bother you."

"It does somewhat, but I don't think it matters. I'm pretty sure that I blew it with her. If you like her, that's fine. I can't say that I blame you. She's beautiful."

"I asked her to go to the movies with me, but she declined. She said that she wants to get settled in and try to make friends."

"I'm glad that I didn't ask her out then. I don't take rejection well."

Matthew laughed and said, "I have to admit, it was driving me crazy watching you flirt with her. I don't think that I've ever been that jealous."

Mark turned his head to look at him. "Why didn't you say something?"

"I don't know. It was awkward for me. It certainly appeared that she liked you. I wasn't sure what to do about it, so I didn't do anything. You know, if she hadn't seen you with Sarah the other night, I think the two of you would've ended up together."

"I know. I made a stupid mistake. I don't know what got into me last week. I acted like a jerk. I hope I can learn from it. As far as Kylie goes, I hope she changes her mind and goes out with you. I think that the two of you would be great together."

Matthew smiled and said, "Thanks. I appreciate that. It's good to see that you're back to your old self again."

"On a different subject, what do you think this meeting is about, tonight?"

"I'm not sure. My parents wouldn't say."

"Do you think that it could be about Emmanuel?"

Matthew nodded and said, "That's what I was thinking. Zeke probably told Pastor Alex."

"What should we tell them?"

"The truth. We haven't done anything wrong, and neither has Emmanuel. Zeke overreacted and our parents will see that. We have nothing to worry about."

Mark nodded in agreement and they left it at that.

When they got to the game, they quickly changed into their uniforms and took the field. Shortly before the game started, Matthew was on the sideline, throwing a ball back and forth with John, getting his arm loose.

Jocelyn came up to the fence and said, "Guess who's here with me."

Matthew glanced over and asked, "Who?"

"Kylie. I gave her a ride. We met at the game Friday night and I offered to bring her here."

Matthew remembered the conversation that he had with Kylie at Sunday school and grasped that Jocelyn was the friend she had referred to. He looked over to her and said, "I asked her out the other day and she turned me down."

"I know. She told me. Don't worry about it. I'm pretty sure that she likes you. She's been asking a lot of questions about you."

"Like what?"

"That's between me and her. I keep telling her what a great guy you are. Hang in there, kiddo. We'll be watching from the stands. Good luck!"

"Thanks."

David hobbled over on his crutches to talk to his girl, while Matthew went back to the bench to watch the opening kickoff.

The game went well. Matthew and Mark both played exceptional again, and it was another easy victory for the Benworth JV squad.

They had a fun ride home, laughing and joking with each other. They were enjoying the win and trying not to worry about the meeting later that night.

Pops was waiting to give them a ride home when they got back to the school. Matthew was wishing that they could walk home, so they might have a chance to see Emmanuel again, but Pops insisted that they ride with him.

As the time for the meeting got closer, Matthew started feeling nervous. He thought about pressing his parents for information during dinner, but chose not to. He would find out soon enough. There was little talk while they ate, which made Matthew even more nervous.

Shortly after dinner, they walked over to Pops' house. They were greeted with a smile. "Phil and Beth, it's always good to see you." He gave Phil a firm handshake and lightly kissed Beth on the cheek.

Mark's parents, Nate and Mary, were already there, along with his older sister, Madison, a junior at the school, and his younger brother, Jacob, who had just begun the first grade.

A few minutes later, John arrived with his parents, Jim and Maggie. Pastor Alex and Zeke were right behind them.

Pastor Alex allowed them to exchange greetings and formalities for a short while, then asked the kids to leave the room so he could talk to the adults in private. He requested that David and Madison stay for the meeting.

Matthew, Mark, Luke and John, along with Jacob, went down into the basement, where Pops had built a very nice game room. They had plenty to do down there while they passed the time. None of them talked about what was going on in the living room above them, but it was on their minds.

—

When the kids went downstairs, Pops closed the door and gave the floor to Pastor Alex.

Alex cleared his throat and began, "I'm sorry to have kept you in the dark these last two days. After service this past Sunday, Zeke came to me with some disturbing news about your kids."

Jim spoke up, "What are you talking about?"

"Maybe it would be best if Zeke told you."

Zeke took a deep breath and said, "First of all, let me apologize for not coming forward sooner. Two Sundays ago, your sons came to me with a story that I found to be unbelievable. Matthew said that while walking through the woods, he jumped across the creek and landed wrong, breaking his ankle."

Phil jumped in, "Matthew's ankle is fine."

"I know. That's where the story gets weird. They claim that a man calling himself Emmanuel came along and healed him."

With a puzzled look on her face, Beth said, "That's insane."

"I agree, but it gets worse. They believe that this guy is Jesus Christ."

Stunned and confused looks filled the room. Nate stood up and said, "I don't think that Mark is that naïve."

"Initially he wasn't. At first, he was just as skeptical as you and me. Then they saw him again this past Saturday. He showed them scars on his wrists and side, just like the ones Jesus had. Now, Mark believes it, too."

They all had concerned looks on their faces. Maggie asked, "Did he tell them that he's Jesus?"

"They said that they figured it out for themselves. When he showed them his scars, I think he made it clear who he's claiming to be. I personally believe that he somehow faked those scars. I don't know who this guy is, but I'm worried about their safety."

Pastor Alex stood up from his chair and paced the room. "I've been running this through my mind ever since Zeke told me about it. At first, I tried to convince myself that the man doesn't exist, that they made the whole thing up. Obviously, you know your kids better than I do, but they don't seem to be the kind of kids to make up a story like this. I think we have to accept the fact that there's a man approaching them in the woods. Of course, he's not Jesus, but we need to find out who he is and what he's up to." He fixed his gaze on David and asked, "Has Matthew told you anything about this?"

"This is the first I've heard about any of this. I'm as surprised as the rest of you."

"How about you, Madison? Has Mark said anything to you?"

"No. Nothing."

"So it appears that Zeke is the only one they've talked to about this. They probably told him because they didn't think that he would tell anyone. That makes me think that they might be hiding something."

Pops said, "We need to assume the worst. He could be a child molester, for all we know."

Alex nodded. "That was the biggest concern of mine. Another thing that crossed my mind was that maybe he's trying to start a cult. That would explain why he's trying to make them believe that he's Jesus. It makes sense that he would target kids, because they're easier to manipulate."

Mary asked, "Do you think that we should tell the police about this guy?"

Pastor Alex replied, "We don't have very much to tell them. We don't even know who this guy is. It's not like the local police have enough manpower to have someone stake out the woods, in the hope that he might show up. Even if he did, there's no law preventing him from being there."

Nate said, "The police could find out who he is. At least we could find out if he has any prior offenses."

Phil said, "Don't get me wrong. I'm just as concerned as the rest of you, but I don't want to make any accusations without proof. I would like to meet this guy and talk to him myself. Do the kids know where he lives?"

Zeke answered, "I don't think so. They say that he appears to them from time to time. They don't look for him. When I press them for more information, they get defensive and clam up."

Phil responded, "Maybe we should bring the kids in here, so we can hear their side of the story."

Alex said, "That's a good idea, but first, let's make sure that we're in agreement on some things. It's important that we get as much information as possible, so that we can make the right decision about how to handle this, but we can't press too hard. Zeke already told us that they get defensive. If we go about this the wrong way, it could be counter productive. We need for them to understand two things. First, that he's not Jesus. Second, that they need to stay clear of him."

Beth asked, "How do we keep them away from him, if he just appears? Zeke told us that they don't go out looking for him."

Jim said, "Well, the only place that they've seen him is in the woods. That makes me believe that he doesn't want anyone to see him talking to the kids. That worries me." He looked at his wife. "What do you think? Should we tell John that he can't go in the woods anymore?"

Maggie answered, "Yeah. I think that's a good idea."

Pastor Alex said, "I think that's an excellent solution. Hopefully, they won't see him anymore, but if they do, it'll most likely be in a public place with witnesses. Then, if he has anything shady planned, he won't be able to execute it. Are we in agreement that we should tell the kids to stay out of the woods from now on?"

They all agreed and decided to bring the kids in to talk to them.

—

The uneasiness in the basement was apparent to all of them. They took turns playing air hockey, but none of them were concentrating on the game.

Matthew asked the others, "Is anyone else nervous about this?"

John answered, "A little." Mark and Luke nodded in agreement.

"I wish we could hear what they were saying."

Luke said, "We'll find out soon enough. Pops has been very quiet the last couple days."

Matthew replied, "So were my folks. Very unusual for them."

Mark said, "I wish that were the case for me. My house is always loud with arguing. I would love to have just one night of silence in my home."

Before anyone could respond, the basement door opened, and Pops called down for them to come upstairs.

At a snail's pace, they filed into the living room and sat on the floor. Pastor Alex started by asking them, "Do you know why we're here tonight?"

Mark glared at Zeke and said, "Yeah. Zeke ratted us out."

Zeke quickly shot back, "Hey! I'm just concerned for your safety."

"Whatever!"

Pastor Alex jumped in, "It's important that we all stay calm. Now, why don't you tell us how you met Emmanuel."

John took the lead, "We were walking home from football practice. We took the shortcut through the woods, like we always do. When we got to the creek, we all jumped over it, but Matthew took a hard landing and broke his ankle. We were trying to help him up, so we could get him home and then to the hospital. Then, Emmanuel came walking down the path and offered to help."

Matthew continued the story, "The pain was really bad. Probably the worst I've ever felt. Emmanuel touched my ankle and I felt heat rushing through it. Within seconds, I felt no more pain."

Phil asked, "Why didn't you tell your mother and me about this?"

"I didn't think that you would believe me."

Beth said, "Please understand, this man didn't heal you. You just didn't hurt yourself as badly as you originally thought."

"My ankle was broken. I heard and felt the bone snap. I told you before that it was the worst pain I'd ever been in."

John added, "I wish that you could've been there to see it. His ankle swelled up to about twice the normal size. As soon as Emmanuel touched him, the swelling went down. I saw it with my own eyes."

David asked, "If this guy has the power to heal, then why didn't you ask him to heal my injury?"

Matthew replied, "I did. He said that he wouldn't, because it wasn't his Father's will."

Pastor Alex said, "You see, that should let you know that he isn't really Jesus. He didn't really heal you and he can't heal anyone else. He used 'his Father's will' as an excuse to hide the fact that he's a fraud."

Mark chimed in, "What about the scars that we saw?"

"Things like that can be done with makeup. Hollywood does it all the time."

John asked, "Then how do you explain the fact that he knows things about our lives that we never told him?"

Looking concerned, his father asked, "Like what?"

"Well, first of all, he knew our names."

Pastor Alex said, "He probably heard you guys talking to each other. It's possible that he was watching you for weeks before showing his face."

John looked frustrated as he said, "He also knew about your conversation with David last week."

David perked up as he asked, "What about it?"

Matthew answered, "He knew that the pastor asked you to forgive Coach King and he knew about the bible that he gave you. How could he have known about these things? He wasn't there."

Pastor Alex said, "He probably overheard you telling your friends about it."

"I didn't say anything about it. In fact, I didn't even know about it. I was in my bedroom doing my homework during your visit."

David appeared to be getting upset as he stared at his younger brother. "Were you eavesdropping on our conversation?"

"No. I just told you that I was in my room doing homework."

"Then how do you know what we talked about?"

"Emmanuel told me."

Phil looked into Matthew's eyes. "I've raised you to tell the truth. If I find out that you're lying about this, I'm going to be very upset with you."

Matthew yelled, "I'm not lying!"

Pastor Alex jumped to his feet and said, "I think we all need to take a deep breath and relax." Looking at Matthew, he continued, "Nobody is calling you a liar. We just want to get to the bottom of this."

Matthew asked, "Then why doesn't anyone believe us?"

Alex answered, "We believe that there is a man calling himself Emmanuel that has been appearing to the four of you in the woods. Our concern is why. It's not normal for a grown man to approach teenage boys."

John said, "He's not dangerous. I don't see what the problem is."

"You have no way of knowing that. He could be establishing trust before his true motives are revealed."

Beth asked, "Has he tried to touch any of you in an inappropriate way?"

Matthew answered back, "No. The first time we saw him, he only touched my ankle when he healed it. The second time, we shook hands, and the third, he gave us all a hug."

Pastor Alex asked, "He hugged you?"

"It was no big deal. It was just a hug."

Phil said, "It is a big deal. What if he tries something more the next time?"

"It's not like that!"

Pastor Alex said, "Maybe. Maybe not. The way he comes to you in the woods is scary. If he has nothing to hide, then why does he only show his face when you're alone in the woods?"

Matthew threw his hands up and said, "You're making him sound like a sick freak. Why are you passing judgment on someone that you haven't even met?"

"We're not passing judgment. The fact that we've never met him is what scares us. We know nothing about this man, and until we do, the four of you need to stay away from him."

John responded, "How are we supposed to do that? We don't go to him. He comes to us."

"Didn't you tell us that the only place that you've seen him is in the woods?"

"Yeah. So?"

Beth said, "We talked about this while you were downstairs, and we agreed that it would be best if you stayed out of the woods from now on. No more shortcuts through the woods and no more riding your bikes in the woods."

Luke was visibly upset. "That shortcut saves us a lot of time."

Pops said, "It's not that much time. I've walked that distance many times myself. If I can handle it at my age, so can you."

John reluctantly said, "Fine. We'll stay out of the woods."

Phil asked, "Can you promise me something?"

Matthew said, "Sure. What?"

"Since you're staying out of the woods, you probably won't see him anymore, but if you do, ask him to meet with us. We would love to ask him some questions."

Pastor Alex added, "Please understand that we're only doing this because we love you and don't want to see you get hurt." He paused for a few seconds, then added, "There's something else that I want you to do for me."

John asked, "What's that?"

"When you get home tonight, go on your computers and put the names Jim Jones and David Koresh into your search engines. Have any of you ever heard of these men?"

They all looked at each other with blank stares. Matthew asked, "Who are they?"

"They were men who deceived many people. They had very loyal followings, and in the end, all of their followers died."

"How did they die?"

"I think that you should research it for yourselves. Then, I think you'll understand why we're so concerned."

The kids agreed to read about these men when they had time and the meeting ended. None of them were happy about how the meeting went. Matthew even had thoughts about ignoring his parents' insistence that he stay out of the woods. He wished that Emmanuel could have been there for the meeting, then the adults would have understood.

—

Matthew went home with his family and logged on to his computer. He read for the next hour or so about Jones and Koresh, horrified by what he learned. So many people, many of them children, died needlessly. Did Pastor Alex really think that Emmanuel was like these men?

He was angry with Pastor Alex and his parents. He wanted to go back into the woods and see Emmanuel. There had to be a way to make them understand.

Frustrated, he went into his bedroom to read his bible. He was surprised to see that it was already opened to the book of Exodus, chapter twenty. He found it odd because he didn't remember leaving it opened, and he had been reading the Gospel of Matthew, not Exodus.

He took a closer look and saw that this was the chapter that contained the Ten Commandments. The fifth commandment, *Honor your father and your mother*, was underlined.

This bible had previously belonged to David, and when he received a new one as a birthday gift a few years earlier, he had given this one to Matthew. He figured that David must have underlined it when it still belonged to him, but he wondered why. He decided to ask him.

In the living room, David was finishing a phone call to Jocelyn. When he hung up, Matthew showed him the bible and asked him, "Why did you underline this passage?"

David looked to where he was pointing and said, "I didn't do that. I've never underlined anything in a bible before."

"Neither have I. I wonder who did it."

David shrugged.

Matthew returned to his bedroom, where he read some more from his bible, then turned out the light. He laid there for quite a while, thinking about whether or not he would go into the woods the next day. He wanted to see Emmanuel again, but couldn't get the fifth commandment out of his mind. The more he thought about it, the more he knew that he couldn't disobey his parents. He would have to stay out of the woods. He hoped that he would see Emmanuel again in some other place, but he had serious doubts that it would happen. He was very sad as he wondered whether or not he would ever see Emmanuel again.

CHAPTER 13

The next morning, Matthew quietly got ready for school. His friends showed up ten minutes earlier than usual to compensate for the extra time that would be needed to get to school on time.

As they walked past *Millie's*, Matthew looked toward the woods, wishing that they could go that way.

The conversation was light for the first few minutes. It seemed like no one wanted to talk about the previous night's meeting. Luke finally asked, "Did anyone look up those guys the pastor told us about last night?"

Matthew and John both said that they did, but Mark shook his head. Luke continued, "I didn't go on the computer, but Pops told me about them. Talk about a couple of nut cases."

Matthew and John laughed in agreement. Mark said, "Fill me in. Who were these guys?"

John answered, "They were both leaders of cults. The first guy, Jim Jones, led a church in California back in the seventies. He took his whole congregation and moved them to South America, where they built their own city. He eventually led them all to kill themselves by drinking *Kool-Aid* laced with cyanide."

Mark asked, "How many died?"

"Over nine hundred. Almost a third of them were kids."

"Why did they go along with it?"

"They were brainwashed."

"What about the other guy?"

Matthew took over. "His name was David Koresh. He believed that he was a prophet and also had a devoted following. They were all living in a compound in Texas when the ATF raided it. A huge standoff ensued, and some agents were killed. The FBI got involved and, when they made their move, a fire broke out in the compound and everyone inside died."

Mark scratched his head. "That's awful. Do you think that Pastor Alex believes that Emmanuel is like those guys?"

"It looks that way."

"He thinks that we're brainwashed?"

Luke said, "I don't know about that, but it's something that we need to think about. What if we really are being deceived?"

Matthew gave him a nasty look. "How can you say that? You were right there when he healed me. You saw the scars."

"I know, but everything they said last night made sense."

"That's because they've never met him."

"I'm not saying that I don't believe, I'm just saying that it wouldn't hurt to be cautious if we ever see him again."

John jumped in, "Look, we don't need to argue about this. It doesn't matter, anyway. We're not allowed back in the woods, so we probably won't ever see him again."

Matthew said, "We could probably get away with going in the woods. As long as we keep it to ourselves, we'll have nothing to worry about."

Luke responded, "No way! Pops was very upset last night after everyone left. He was adamant that I never go into the woods again. I'm not taking the chance of facing that wrath."

John said, "My folks were the same way. My dad even considered calling the principal, so he could warn all the kids about going into the woods, but my mom talked him out of it."

Luke looked at Mark and asked, "What did your parents say about it?"

He answered, "They didn't say anything to me. They were too busy arguing with each other. That's why I didn't go on the computer. I've learned that when they're fighting, it's best to stay out of the way. I locked myself in my room and listened to some music to drown out the sounds of their bickering."

Luke asked, "Do they argue a lot?"

"All the time. I'm getting nervous that they might get divorced."

"What do they fight about?"

Matthew gave Luke a look and shook his head, letting him know that he didn't think he should be asking him that.

Mark didn't seem to notice as he answered, "All kinds of things. Sometimes I think that they argue just for the sake of arguing. They just don't seem to like each other, anymore."

The other three saw the tears in Mark's eyes. Matthew wanted to say something that might help him, but decided that it would be best if he kept his mouth shut.

The subject switched to the upcoming football game against Allegheny Hills, scheduled for Friday night. They all agreed that Cody would have to improve his play if they were to have a chance of winning. Allegheny Hills won their first two games, decisively, and the local newspaper had them ranked number seven in the state. They all had their doubts that they could win. If they couldn't beat lowly Westfield, then they didn't stand a chance against a powerhouse like Allegheny Hills.

When they got to school, they took their usual seats in the cafeteria. Tim joined them shortly after.

As they talked, Tim repeatedly rubbed his left shoulder, grimacing each time. Matthew couldn't help but see the alarmed look on John's face.

Just before the bell rang, Matthew saw Kylie sitting a few tables away, talking with some other freshman girls. He watched her and was pleased that she was making friends so quickly. She looked over and caught him staring. She smiled and gave him a little wave. He smiled back, then blushed and looked away.

He saw her again in history and biology class, where they engaged in small talk before class began. He was feeling more and more confident every time he talked to her.

He thought about talking to her again during lunch, but she seemed to be having a great time with her friends, so he stayed at his own table with his friends. He didn't want to scare her off by coming on too strong.

School ended and practice began. Coach King was working them harder than normal. He was upset about last week's loss to Westfield. He was really pressuring Cody to play better, but it was having the opposite effect. Cody's passes continued to be off target, and the rest of the offense was losing what was left of their dwindling confidence.

Even Dylan and Hunter, who had been Cody's biggest defenders the previous week, were becoming visibly annoyed with him. Matthew overheard Hunter say to Dylan, "This really sucks! We're seniors. This is our last year and we get stuck with this lousy quarterback."

Dylan responded, "I know. If David hadn't gotten hurt, we would've won easily last week. Do you know how many times I was wide open and he couldn't get the ball to me? We could've won state this year, but now we'll be lucky to win another game, let alone make the playoffs."

"Maybe we should talk to the coach about letting Matthew play. He couldn't possibly do any worse."

A smile crossed Matthew's face. Knowing that his brother's friends believed in him did wonders for his self esteem.

For the last fifteen minutes of practice, Matthew worked with the first team offense. His passes were precise and the rest of the team took notice. After each completion, he looked to the coach to gage his reaction. Coach King kept a poker face, but Matthew knew that he was making an impression on him.

At the end of practice, Matthew walked with John and Tim to the locker room. As he walked in, he made eye contact with Cody, who gave him a dirty look. Matthew looked away quickly. He didn't want any problems. They were on the same team, after all.

While they were taking their equipment off, John looked over at Tim as he took off his shoulder pads. There was a big bruise on his left shoulder, in the same place that they saw him rubbing that morning. John nudged Matthew and motioned for him to follow. They walked over to Tim's locker, where John asked, "What happened to your shoulder?"

Tim looked down and said, "Oh that? It's nothing. I woke up in the middle of the night and had to use the bathroom. I didn't turn on the light, so I couldn't see very well. When I walked into the bathroom, I slammed my shoulder into the doorframe."

John and Matthew looked at each other. Matthew didn't believe him and it was obvious that John didn't either. Matthew said, "Turn the light on next time."

Tim laughed nervously and continued changing.

John and Matthew went back to their own lockers where John said, "He's lying. I know he is. You don't get a bruise that big from bumping into a wall."

"I agree. What should we do?"

"I don't know. I wish we could talk to Emmanuel."

"Me too. Do you want to go through the woods anyway? Our parents will probably never find out."

John paused for a few seconds before responding, "I would love to, but we better not. I can only imagine how long I would be grounded for if we got caught."

"Yeah. Me too. Do you think we'll ever see him again?"

"I've been thinking about that a lot since last night. I hope we do, of course, but I have serious doubts."

They finished changing in silence, then went outside where Tim was about to leave for home. He lived in the opposite direction, so they wouldn't be walking together. John gave him a fist bump and said, "You have my phone number. You can call me anytime, for any reason."

Tim nodded, but didn't say anything as he turned and started walking home.

Mark and Luke came out of the locker room and joined them as they started their jaunt home. They talked sparingly until they reached the entrance into the woods.

Matthew halted and stared down the path. The other three kept walking a few steps until they realized that he had stopped.

Luke said, "Come on, Matthew. You know we can't go in there."

"What if Emmanuel is waiting for us?"

John answered, "Then he'll be waiting for a long time. We've already discussed this. We're not going that way anymore."

Feeling frustrated, Matthew stormed past them down the sidewalk, and said, "Let's get going."

John rushed ahead to catch up, with Mark and Luke close behind. Nobody said anything for the next couple of minutes.

They approached a bus stop, where they saw a man with a gray hoodie sitting on the bench with his hood pulled up over his head. When they got to him, he pulled down the hood, revealing his identity.

It was Emmanuel!

Matthew recognized him immediately and exclaimed, "I can't believe it's you."

Emmanuel returned the greeting with a big smile and a hug. One at a time, the other three hugged him too.

John said, "I wasn't sure if we would ever see you again. Our parents won't let us go into the woods anymore. They think that you're a fraud and they're worried that you might try to hurt us."

Emmanuel nodded and said, "I know. I want to reassure the four of you that I would never do anything to harm you."

Matthew said, "We know. Our parents are just being paranoid."

"No, they're not. Their concern just shows how much they love you."
He paused briefly, then said, "Let's talk for a few minutes."

Matthew sat on the bench to his right, with John to the left. Mark and
Luke stayed on their feet, facing them.

Emmanuel looked Luke in the eye and said, "Don't worry about the
doubts that you're having. It's perfectly normal to face doubt from time
to time."

Luke stared at the ground. "Everything that Pops said last night made
sense. He had me convinced that you're a fake."

"Pops believes in me, he just has a hard time believing that I'm who
you say I am. Don't let it get you down. If you had never met me and
someone else told you the same story that you told last night, would you
believe it?"

Luke shook his head. "Probably not."

"So don't be so hard on your folks. Not many would ever believe this,
including yourselves."

Matthew said, "I seriously considered going into the woods even
though our parents forbid it."

"You made the right decision by not going in there. It's very important
to be obedient to your parents. That is the fifth commandment, you
know."

"My bible was opened to that page last night. That passage in
particular was underlined. I asked my brother if he did it, but he said that
he didn't."

Emmanuel just smiled at him.

Matthew continued by asking, "Did you have anything to do with
that?"

"Don't worry about it. The important thing is that you listened to your
folks. If you hadn't, you wouldn't have seen me because I was waiting for
you here. What you're not aware of, is that if you had gone into the woods,
you would have had trouble that you're not prepared for."

John asked, "Would our parents have found out?"

"Worse. Jude, Scott and Ethan are in there, as we speak. They're
waiting for the four of you to come through, and believe me, they have
bad intentions."

Shocked looks came across all four of their faces. Mark said, "I guess
we're lucky that our parents reacted the way they did."

"Luck had nothing to do with it. Your parents weren't the only ones
who wanted you to stay out of the woods. I did, too."

Matthew asked, "Why do you want us to stay out?"

"It can be dangerous. Jude and his friends are waiting to ambush you. Stay alert at all times, especially when you're alone."

Luke said, "Those guys are jerks! What should we do about them?"

"Pray for them."

"Pray for them? I don't even like them. Why would I want to pray for them?"

"Matthew 5:44 says, 'Love your enemies and pray for those who persecute you.'"

John said, "That has always confused me. How can you love your enemy? It seems impossible."

Emmanuel sighed. "What you need to understand is that the word love has more than one meaning. Most of the time, love is a feeling. The way that you love your family and friends is a feeling. However, in this context, it is not a feeling, but an action. Praying for someone is an excellent way to show love."

Mark shook his head. "I'm going to be honest with you. I don't want to pray for them. Those guys have been giving us a hard time for years."

"I'm aware of all the things that they've done, and I'm not happy with how they live their lives, but this might surprise you. I love them as much as I love you. I know that they can change and repent. I'm asking the four of you to pray for them."

Luke asked, "Is there anything in particular that you want us to pray for?"

"Trust the Holy Spirit to guide your prayers."

After about fifteen seconds of silence, Emmanuel continued, "I think that we need to address a potential problem between two of you. It appears that Matthew and Mark are interested in the same girl."

Mark laughed and said, "It's not a problem. As soon as I found out that Matthew liked her, I made the decision to back off. I wish that he would have said something sooner. If I had known, I never would have pursued her in the first place."

Emmanuel smiled and said, "That's very mature of you, Mark. If Kylie decides to date Matthew, are you going to be okay with that?"

"Yeah. It's not like I'm in love with her or anything. I just think she's cute and had fun flirting with her. I'm actually hoping that she goes out with him. I think that they'll make a great couple."

"I'm glad that you feel that way." Addressing Matthew, he continued, "Don't give up on her, but go slow. She doesn't need a boyfriend right now. What she needs is a good friend. I want you to be that friend."

Grinning from ear to ear, Matthew said, "I can do that. Anyway, I'm not sure that I have time for a relationship right now. Between football practice and my school work, I don't have very much free time. Maybe when football season is over."

"Speaking of football, keep working hard at practice. You need to be ready when your time to play arises. Your time is coming."

"What do you mean?"

"Just be ready."

John looked troubled as he said, "I don't mean to change the subject, but I'm really worried about Tim. He has another bruise, and when I asked him about it, he said that he walked into a doorframe. I didn't believe him for a second."

Emmanuel put his arm around John's shoulder and said, "I'm very pleased with how well you're handling this situation. Even though Tim lied to you today, he's starting to trust you. Keep doing what you're doing."

"I feel like I'm not doing enough. I don't want to see him get hurt anymore."

"Neither do I, but if you pry into his personal life too soon, he'll push you away. Be patient, and in time, he'll reveal the truth to you. In the meantime, be the friend that he needs."

"Being his friend is the easy part. He's a really great guy and I love hanging out with him."

"I know. Pray for his father. He's in desperate need of prayer."

"I have been. There's one other thing that I want to talk to you about. At the meeting last night, Matthew's father told us that if we ever saw you again, that we should ask you to meet our folks. Are you willing to meet with them?"

Emmanuel ran his fingers through his hair and took a deep breath. "The problem is that they have already made up their minds about me. They won't believe anything I tell them. For that reason, I won't meet with them. Please understand that a meeting with them would do more harm than good."

Luke asked, "Should we tell them that we saw you today?"

"That's up to you." Emmanuel looked up the street as the sound of a bus drew near. It pulled up to the curb as Emmanuel said, "Well, this is my bus. You guys take care of yourselves. Keep reading your bibles and pray hard."

John asked, "Where are you going?"

"I have places that I need to be."

Matthew asked, "When will we see you again?"

"Just keep your eyes open. I'll be around."

Emmanuel disappeared inside the bus. They waved as the bus rode off down the street.

—

An hour later, Jude, Scott and Ethan came out of the woods. They were angry about waiting so long, without the kids showing up.

Jude told his friends that they needed to change their method. He said that instead of waiting in the woods, they would try to find some other places, when they are alone, not all together.

Jude had something specific in mind, and when he told Scott and Ethan, they smiled and eagerly awaited the next day when they would execute the plan.

CHAPTER 14

Mark sat quietly on the sofa, pretending to be interested in the TV show that his sister, Madison, was watching. He could hear his parents arguing in the kitchen. Their fighting was becoming repetitive. His dad lost too much money betting on football games, and his mom spent too much money on clothes. They would go back and forth, neither of them wanting to admit that they were wrong.

He finally had enough. It was twenty minutes before he was planning to leave, but he couldn't take their bickering anymore. He picked up his bible and left the house without even bothering to say goodbye. His parents knew that he was going to the church for the Thursday night youth group. They probably wouldn't even notice that he was gone because they were so consumed by the argument they were having.

Mark walked along Forest Street toward Luke and Pops' house, where everyone was meeting. From there, Pops would give them a ride to the church.

As he was about to pass a van that was parked along the curb, Jude stepped in front of him, having been waiting out of sight in front of the van. Mark stopped in his tracks. He backed up a step, then turned around to run the other way. As he did, Ethan appeared from behind the van. Mark thought about running up to a neighbor's house to seek help, but just then, Scott came out of hiding from behind a tree in the nearest yard.

He was boxed in!

Mark said, "I don't want any trouble."

"I don't care what you want," said Jude, with a sneer.

They closed in on him. Mark tried to run past Ethan, but was tackled to the ground. He scrambled to his feet, but was quickly grabbed from behind by Scott. Mark wriggled and squirmed, trying to break free, but

Scott was too strong for him. While Scott held him from behind, Jude punched him twice in the stomach, taking all the air out of his lungs. The next punch was in the mouth, cutting his lip, followed by another to the nose, drawing blood from his nostril.

Mark crumbled to the ground in the grass next to the sidewalk, where all three took turns kicking and stomping him. He curled his body into a fetal position, hoping it would end soon.

The owner of the house they were in front of, an elderly man that Mark knew as Mr. McNeil, opened his front door and yelled out, "Leave him alone."

The beating stopped as Jude called back, "Shut up, old man, or you'll get the same!"

Mr. McNeil shouted back. "Leave now, or I'm calling the police."

Jude bent down and grabbed a handful of Mark's hair, jerking his head up. "The next time you and your friends decide to give me a hard time, it'll be worse. Do you understand? Tell your buddies that we'll be watching for them."

Picking up Mark's bible, which had fallen to the ground during the melee, Jude started ripping pages out, crumbling them up, and grinding them into the ground with his shoe. He took what was left of the bible and threw it down an open sewer grate, by the curb.

They left Mark there, coughing and spitting blood from his mouth. Mr. McNeil came out and helped him to his feet. Feeling embarrassed, Mark assured him that he was fine and denied the help that was offered. He continued down the street toward Pops' house.

When he got there, Pops answered the door. "What happened?"

"Jude and his friends roughed me up."

Pops led him to the bathroom to clean up. When the blood was cleaned off of his face, it became apparent that he was going to have a large fat lip. Pops gave him some ice wrapped up in a towel to help with the swelling.

Pops called his parents while Mark sat down on the sofa beside Luke. His ribs were aching pretty bad, a result of the many kicks and stomps he received. Taking the phone from Pops, he told his mom and dad that he was fine. They asked him to come home, but he said that he really wanted to go to youth group, so they relented.

After hanging up, he told Pops about his bible being destroyed and thrown down the sewer, so Pops gave him an extra one that he had and told him that he could keep it.

Matthew arrived and John followed shortly thereafter. They listened to Mark's story about the beating and about Jude's warning for the rest of them. After discussing the situation for a few minutes, they agreed that it would be best if, whenever possible, they would stick together when walking around the neighborhood.

When it was time to leave, they all got into the minivan with Pops behind the wheel. They swung by Tim's house to pick him up, then headed to the church.

Mark gingerly walked in to the youth center and sat down, holding his ribs. Seeing this, and noticing his fat lip, Zeke came over and asked him what happened. Mark told him about the attack.

Looking at him skeptically, Zeke asked, "Who are these guys?"

"Just some troublemakers that live in our neighborhood. They don't attend this church, so you probably don't know them."

"Did Emmanuel do this to you?"

"No. I already told you who did it."

"Have you stayed out of the woods?"

"Of course." Mark was getting flustered.

Zeke let it go, but it was clear that he doubted Mark's story.

—

The Thursday night group kept all the high school kids together, regardless of what grade they were in. This meant that Tim could stay with them. He sat next to John where they talked and joked together like friends who'd known each other for years.

More kids were filing in, as the time to get started approached. Just as Zeke announced that everyone should take their seats, Kylie walked in. She and Matthew made eye contact. They smiled at each other, and she went over and sat next to him.

Dylan and Hunter were sitting in the row behind them and made a couple comments to Matthew, trying to embarrass him. It worked. Kylie just smiled and enjoyed the attention.

Zeke began by teaching a lesson from the book of Exodus. He taught about the Israelites' escape from Egypt and how Passover began.

When the lesson was over, Zeke went to the CD player to start the worship segment of the night. He put on the *Take Everything* CD by Seventh Day Slumber, which consisted of hard rock versions of popular worship songs. He was having a problem getting it to work, which gave Matthew and Kylie a chance to talk for a few minutes.

Kylie asked, "What happened to Mark?"

"There's some older kids in our neighborhood who have been giving us a hard time. They caught him alone today and roughed him up a little."

"Is he alright?"

"He's fine. I think his fat lip is an improvement."

She laughed and gave him a small shove. She added, with a hint of sarcasm, "That's real nice to say about your friend."

Matthew laughed with her for a few seconds, then got serious. "I'm a little nervous about bringing this up, but it looked like you were interested in him last week. In fact, up until you saw him flirting with Sarah at Mario's last Friday, I thought for sure that you two would end up together. Do you feel anything for him?"

"Not really. Keep in mind that I'm new around here. I wasn't looking forward to starting over at a new school. I've never been 'the new kid' before, so on the first day of school, when he started flirting with me, it made me feel good. I was so afraid that nobody would like me. He made me feel accepted right away."

"You looked pretty mad at Mario's."

"I was, at first, but I knew all along that I wasn't going to date him, so I got over it pretty quick. I'd still like to be his friend. He's a really funny guy."

"Yes, he is. We've been friends for a long time."

"You said that you were nervous about bringing it up. Why?"

Matthew took a deep breath and said, "Because, I like you."

She smiled. "I like you, too, but I'm not ready for anything romantic just yet. Let's just keep it as friends for now, and get to know each other better. I'm going to pray about this, and I ask you to do the same, and we'll see where God leads us."

"I can do that."

Zeke got the CD player working and they all got to their feet to worship.

After a few songs, the game room was opened. This room consisted of two ping pong tables, two air hockey tables, and a pool table. Each week at youth group, after the lesson and worship were finished, the kids would get an hour to play and socialize.

This was Kylie's first night attending the youth group, so she hadn't seen the game room yet. She asked Matthew to accompany her to the room and show her around, and he was happy to oblige. She challenged him to a game of air hockey, and he accepted.

Matthew's first thought was to go easy on her, since he considered himself a pretty good player, but when Kylie took an early 3-0 lead, he quickly learned that she wasn't a pushover. He started playing harder and in no time, the score was tied.

Kylie said, "You're good at this."

"Luke has a table in his grandfather's basement. We play all the time."

"I've got quite a bit of experience myself." She added with a wink, "I hope you know that I allowed you to score those last three goals, just to make it interesting."

Matthew's eyes got big. "Oh, really?"

"Yes. You can't beat me."

"We'll see about that."

"Would you care to make a wager?"

"Name it."

Kylie thought about it and said, "The loser pays for pizza tomorrow night at Mario's. That is, if you plan on going there after the game."

"I'm definitely going now. I never pass up free pizza."

They both laughed and continued with the game.

—

When the worship ended, Luke and Mark stayed in the classroom talking about what had happened earlier with Jude and his friends. Luke asked him if he was hurt. Mark told him that he was more embarrassed than anything else. He wasn't looking forward to explaining his fat lip to everyone at school the next day.

Luke got up from where he was sitting and went over to the window. He looked outside and called Mark over. "I think Emmanuel is out there."

Mark ran over to see for himself. Sure enough, there was Emmanuel, leaning against a utility pole near the entrance into the parking lot.

Mark went to the other room to tell the others. He saw Matthew playing air hockey with Kylie. John and Tim were at the pool table, playing doubles against Dylan and Hunter. They looked like they were having a good time, so he didn't say anything to them.

He looked over to where Zeke was sitting. He was engaged in a conversation with some underclassmen and wasn't paying attention to Mark and Luke. They took advantage of this and quietly slipped outside.

They walked straight to Emmanuel and were greeted with a smile. He looked at Mark and said, "I'm sorry about what happened to you, today."

"It's no big deal."

"Are you hurt?"

"This fat lip is embarrassing. I don't want to have to explain it to everybody at school tomorrow. My ribs and back are sore from where they kicked me. I'm just worried that if I get the chance to play in the game tomorrow night, I'll be too sore."

Emmanuel placed his hands on each side of Mark's head and looked to the sky. Luke watched in amazement as the swelling of Mark's bottom lip went down in a matter of seconds. Emmanuel lowered his hands to Mark's side and did the same thing. He repeated the process by putting his hands on Mark's back.

When he was finished, Mark felt no more pain. "Thank you."

"You're welcome."

"So, you really did heal Matthew's ankle. That was the one thing I had a hard time believing."

Emmanuel nodded and asked, "Did you pray for Jude and his friends, like I asked you to?"

Mark shook his head while Luke said, "I did."

"I know you did, Luke. So did Matthew and John. Why didn't you, Mark?"

"Because, I don't like them."

"I'm not asking you to like them. I'm asking you to pray for them. Can you do that?"

Mark was pacing around the parking lot, getting frustrated, "Of course I can. I'm just not sure that I want to."

Switching his attention to Luke, Emmanuel asked, "What did you pray for?"

"I remembered that you told me to allow the Holy Spirit to direct my prayer, so I prayed for God's will to be done in their lives. I asked for conviction to fall on their hearts every time they do something wrong. I prayed for people to be put in their paths that will lead them to God."

Emmanuel nodded his approval. He looked back to Mark and asked, "Does that sound hard to you?"

Mark looked to the ground and said, "No. I'll start praying for them." He picked his head up and said, "I'm worried about my parents. They fight a lot and I'm getting scared that they might get divorced. What can I do?"

"You can start by not giving them a hard time when they ask you to do things around the house. You're not helping the situation when you're disobedient to them. Also, try to get along better with Madison. If you can have a better relationship with your sister, it could rub off on your parents. Your little brother is important to this, too. I don't think you know just how much Jacob looks up to you. You'll be doing wonders for him if you can be a good role model."

Mark was astonished. "I worry about Jacob a lot. Every time my parents argue, he goes to his room and cries. I want to say something to help, but I can never think of anything."

"You don't have to say anything. Just be with him. Offer to play a game with him, or read a story to him. You could even help him with his school work. He loves spending time with you, so any of these things will be helpful."

Tears filled Mark's eyes as he hugged Emmanuel. "Thank you."

Emmanuel hugged Luke and said, "You guys better get back inside before Zeke notices that you're gone. Tell Matthew and John that I'm sorry I missed them, and give this message to Matthew. Tell him to be ready to play tomorrow night."

Luke asked, "Is he going to play?"

"Just tell him to be ready."

Emmanuel turned around and walked down the street, out of their sight.

Luke and Mark returned to the youth center. As they went inside, Zeke saw them and called out, "Where were you two?"

Luke answered, "We were hot, so we went outside to get some fresh air."

Zeke got up and ran to the door. He looked around outside. "Was there anyone else out there?"

Mark smirked and asked, "Do you see anyone out there?"

"You know the rules. You're not allowed outside."

"We know. We won't do it again."

Zeke squinted as he looked at Mark. "Your fat lip is gone. What happened?"

Mark shrugged his shoulders, but didn't say anything. Zeke gave him a disbelieving look, but said nothing as he returned to where he was sitting.

—

When the parents started arriving to pick up the kids, Zeke called them together and closed out the night with a prayer.

Kylie's dad pulled up in his car. Matthew and Kylie hugged. She said, "I'll see you tomorrow night at Mario's. Don't forget to bring your money."

Matthew smiled and said, "You won't get so lucky next time."

She smiled back and said, "Luck had nothing to do with it." She reached over and slipped a piece of paper into his hand.

"What's this?"

She leaned close to whisper, "My phone number. Call me anytime." She turned around and got into the car.

He watched as they drove out of the parking lot, then he returned to his friends. They were sitting near the door, waiting for Pops. Tim was on the other side of the room, talking with Hunter and Dylan.

John asked Matthew, "What's up with you and Kylie?"

"Nothing. We're just friends. I'm going to follow Emmanuel's advice and be friends first."

Luke said, "Speaking of Emmanuel, you missed him tonight."

Matthew asked, "He was here?"

Mark answered, "Yep. He was out in the parking lot while you guys played in here. We went out and he healed my injuries. He also gave me some good advice about my family problems."

Luke added, "He wants us to give you a message. He said to be ready to play tomorrow night."

Matthew was speechless as Pops rolled up in the minivan. They all climbed in and enjoyed great fellowship during the ride home. Matthew was pleased with the way that things seemed to be working out. He was happy about how well he and Kylie were getting along. He was also glad that he and Mark were in agreement about her. Knowing that Mark was okay with the possibility that he and Kylie might date someday made him rest easy.

When they dropped Mark off in front of his house, Matthew smiled to himself. He was overjoyed that his friend was back to his old self.

—

Mark went inside his house and told his parents what happened.

His dad commented, "Your face looks okay. Pops told us that you were marked up. A fat lip and some bruises."

Mark brushed it aside and lied, "You know how Pops exaggerates. It wasn't that bad." He knew that he couldn't tell them that Emmanuel healed him.

His mom said, "Well, the important thing is that you're alright."

Although they were showing concern and were thankful that he wasn't hurt, Mark could see the distraction on their faces. The lingering effects from their argument still hung in the air. He decided that it would be best to leave them alone to work things out.

He went to Jacob's room where his little brother was coloring a picture that he had drawn. Jacob was thrilled when Mark raved about how good it was.

It was getting close to Jacob's bedtime, so Mark took a book off the bookshelf and read Jacob's favorite story to him until he fell asleep. He tucked him in, turned out the light, and quietly closed the door.

Returning to his own bedroom, he took the bible that Pops had given him and sat at his desk. He had never read it on his own before, so he wasn't sure where to start. He thought to himself that the beginning was as good a place as any. He opened the bible to the book of Genesis and began reading.

He quickly got lost in God's Word as he read about how the world was created. He wasn't sure how long he read, but eventually, his eyes got heavy. He placed a bookmark on the page and closed the bible.

He got up from his desk and walked over to his bed, where he dropped to his knees. He prayed for his parents, hoping that God would intervene and save their marriage. He prayed for Tim, asking God to protect him from his father. He prayed for all of his family and friends, individually, asking for blessings over their lives. Lastly, he prayed for Jude, Scott and Ethan.

He slept better that night than he could ever remember.

CHAPTER 15

The Benworth Eagles left the locker room and ran out onto the field. The crowd gave them a nice ovation. The bleachers were packed, as usual.

The support for the Allegheny Hills Grizzlies was just as strong, as their fans made the trip to see their team play on the road. Blue and white pompoms, matching their uniforms, were being waved throughout their stands.

Just before the opening kickoff, Luke said to Matthew, "Remember what Emmanuel said. Be ready to play."

"I'm ready."

Cody heard this and gave Matthew a cold look. He shrugged it off and searched the stands for Kylie. He spotted her sitting with Jocelyn. In the row behind them, was Emmanuel. Matthew laughed to himself and wondered if the girls had any clue that their Lord and Savior was sitting right behind them.

—

Tim placed the ball on the kicking tee, backed up ten yards, and counted the players to make sure that they had eleven players on the field. When he was sure that everyone was ready, he raised his right hand, signaling to the officials that he was ready to go. The referee blew his whistle and Tim kicked the ball high into the western Pennsylvania sky.

The deep man for Allegheny Hills caught the ball at his goal line. With a burst of speed, he found a seam up the middle and Benworth scrambled to catch him. Just past midfield, he had only Tim to beat. Not having much football experience, Tim looked shaky as the return man ran toward him. In desperation, Tim threw his body into his opponents legs, taking his feet out from under him. The Grizzlies would start their first drive from the Eagles forty yard line.

The Benworth defense, who had been solid the first two games, took the field. This would be their toughest test, so far. In the previous two games, Allegheny Hills had scored a total of eighty-six points in their blowout wins. A much better offense than Valley Prep and Westfield.

Using a good mix of runs and passes, they kept the Eagles defense off balance, methodically moving the ball downfield. On a third and goal from the five, Allegheny Hills quarterback found his tight end on a slant pass for the first touchdown of the game.

Groans and complaints filled the Benworth bleachers. Any confidence that the Eagles sideline had, went away in a hurry. After the extra point, they trailed 7-0.

Hunter returned the ensuing kickoff to the Eagles forty yard line. Cody looked timid as he approached the line of scrimmage for his first play. The Allegheny Hills defense was big and intimidating. The first few plays were runs, with Hunter picking up good yardage each time. After two first downs, they had advanced the ball inside their opponents' thirty yard line.

The next two plays only netted three yards, so, on third down, they called a pass play. Cody couldn't find an open receiver, so he dumped the ball off to Hunter in the flats. He turned up field and was brought down two yards shy of a first down.

Tim was called on to kick a field goal and the Grizzlies lead was cut to 7-3.

The kick return man didn't have as much success the second time around, as he was wrapped up at the twenty-five yard line.

Once again, the Eagles defense struggled. Allegheny Hills made it look easy as they drove down the field. Before long, they were inside the Eagles twenty yard line. The defense tightened up the next two plays, forcing a third and long. The third down pass fell incomplete and they had to settle for a field goal, increasing their lead to 10-3.

The next Eagles possession produced nothing. After two short runs and an incomplete pass, they punted.

Allegheny Hills picked up two first downs before their next drive stalled. Their punter did an excellent job angling the kick to the sideline, as the ball went out of bounds at the one yard line, ending the first quarter.

Benworth tried playing it safe by running the ball, but the defense was ready for it and stuffed the first two plays for no gain. On third down, Cody dropped back to pass. Dylan was open fifteen yards downfield, but Cody hesitated. The blitz came from his blind side and he was sacked in the end zone for a safety, giving Allegheny Hills a 12-3 lead.

The usually mild mannered Dylan showed his frustration by slamming his helmet to the ground when he got to the sideline.

The Eagles defense came up big on the next drive, forcing a fumble and recovering the ball, but Cody gave the ball right back by throwing an interception on the next play.

As the second quarter dragged on, the Benworth team got more and more discouraged, as it became apparent that they were overmatched. Several players voiced their disdain about how the season was a lost cause without David in the lineup.

Just before halftime, Allegheny Hills added a field goal to give them a 15-3 lead.

—

Back in the locker room, Coach King was furious. As a Christian man, he usually prided himself on keeping his temper in check, but this night was different. He released a tirade that surprised most of the players. He was extremely upset with Cody. He singled him out as he screamed in his face, "You'd better get your act together, or your butt will be right back on the bench."

Matthew felt a rush of excitement go through his blood, but tried not to show it. He silently prayed to get himself mentally prepared to play while the coach berated the team. He made eye contact with David, who was leaning on his crutches behind the coach. David gave him a nod as if to say, *you can do this.*

Cody looked defeated as he slumped in his seat across the room. Matthew felt pity for him, but at the same time, he wanted to win. He didn't think that they stood a chance of winning with Cody playing quarterback. He wanted the chance.

The offense showed some signs of life as the second half began. Cody completed two passes to Dylan and Hunter broke free for some big gains, putting the ball deep into Allegheny Hills territory, but they couldn't complete the drive. Cody's third down pass sailed over Dylan's head, so Tim came out for his second field goal of the night, cutting the deficit to 15-6.

The Eagles defense stiffened in the second half, forcing Allegheny Hills to punt on their next two possessions, but they couldn't capitalize and had to punt the ball right back to them.

As the third quarter was winding down, hope was restored to the Benworth faithful when an Eagles defender intercepted a pass and returned it to the Allegheny Hills fifteen yard line. Cody and the offense came out fired up. On the next two plays, Hunter picked up three yards each time. On third down, Cody faked the handoff to Hunter and ran a bootleg to the right. Dylan was the primary receiver, but he was double covered. Cody saw an open receiver to his left and threw the ball across the field. The ball was severely under thrown and intercepted. Cody gave chase, but couldn't catch him, as the interception was returned for a touchdown.

As the final seconds of the third quarter ticked away, the Eagles trailed 22-6.

—

Coach King threw his clipboard to the ground. His eyes searched the sideline as he called out, "Matthew Peters! Get over here!"

Matthew immediately ran to the coach where he was asked, "Are you ready to play?"

"Yes, sir!" Adrenaline ran through Matthew's veins. He couldn't wait to get out there and prove to everyone that he was the right player for the job. Knowing that Emmanuel and Kylie were watching from the crowd just energized him more.

The coach put his hands on Matthew's shoulder pads and said, "Listen to me. We have no choice but to abandon the running game. We're down by sixteen and there's not much time left. We can't afford any more mistakes. I need you to step up and take control of this game. Can you do that?"

"You know I can, Coach!"

Cody saw them talking and ran over to hear what they were talking about. Coach King turned to him and said, "Have a seat. You're done for the night."

"What are you talking about? You can't take me out of the game."

"I can and I will. Matthew is going to finish the game."

Rage filled Cody's eyes as he pleaded with the coach. "You're replacing me with a freshman? He can't handle this. That defense will eat him alive!"

"My decision is made. Sit down!"

Cody reluctantly walked away and sulked on the bench.

The coach turned to Matthew and said, "I have confidence in you. Don't let me down."

"I won't."

After the kickoff, the Eagles had the ball on the twenty-eight yard line. Matthew ran onto the field and a cheer erupted from the Benworth bleachers.

—

Kylie and Jocelyn jumped to their feet when they saw Matthew running onto the field. Kylie yelled, "It's about time!"

The fans livened up when they saw Matthew enter the game. They had been complaining about Cody's play all night.

Kylie heard an older gentleman in the row in front of her say, "Let's hope that he's as good as his brother."

The excitement that she felt kept her fidgety. Her stomach was in knots as she tried to sit still. She wanted Matthew to play well. She wondered how nervous he was, as she was plenty nervous for the both of them.

Jocelyn put her arm around Kylie's shoulder and said, "Relax. He's going to do fine."

"I hope he doesn't get hurt. Those guys are so much bigger than he is."

"Let's pray for him."

They leaned into each other and quietly prayed for Matthew's safety. Sitting in the row behind them, a man in a gray hoodie smiled his approval.

Matthew called the first play in the huddle, then lined up in the shotgun formation. He took the snap and quickly connected with Dylan for a twelve yard gain.

Two more completions put the ball on the Allegheny Hills thirty-five yard line. A buzz was stirring on the Benworth side of the field. The Grizzlies defense was getting rattled and their fans were getting worried.

The next play, Matthew couldn't find an open receiver. The protection from the offensive line was giving way, so he took off running up the middle. He juked a linebacker and cut to the right, where he was forced out of bounds, but not until he had picked up twenty yards. The Benworth fans were on their feet cheering.

The Allegheny Hills defense was on their heels. Matthew took advantage of this on the next play by throwing a high pass into the left corner of the end zone, where Dylan out-jumped his defender and came down with the ball for a touchdown.

After Tim kicked the extra point, they trailed 22-13. Several players congratulated Matthew, but Cody glared at him from the bench. Matthew was too excited to let it bother him. He also knew that they had a long way to go, so he needed to stay focused.

Allegheny Hills got the ball back and started their next drive. The Benworth defense showed signs of fatigue as they gave up a few first downs. The clock kept ticking, and by the time they forced a punt, there was just over four minutes left to play. To make matters worse, they had only one timeout left due to Cody wasting two in the third quarter to avoid delay of game penalties.

They punted the ball over Hunter's head and downed it at the five yard line. The Benworth fans were trying to stay optimistic, but doubt was creeping in.

Matthew went to the huddle and tried to rally the offense. "Come on, guys! We can do this!"

Dylan said, "Utilize the sidelines, so we can stop the clock. If nobody's open, throw the ball out of bounds. Don't force anything."

Matthew nodded and called the play. He led them on a drive that was close to perfect. His passes were on target and they quickly moved the ball downfield. Unfortunately, the clock was not on their side. They got the ball down to the Allegheny Hills fifteen yard line with 1:32 left in the game.

Matthew's next pass was completed to Dylan at the eight yard line, but he was tackled before he could get out of bounds. The clock kept ticking as they waited for the official to spot the ball. Matthew was shouting to the offense to line up as quickly as possible. They finally got lined up and Matthew spiked the ball, stopping the clock with fifty-six seconds remaining.

On third down, Allegheny Hills blitzed and before Matthew could get the ball away, he was sacked. The clock kept moving. They had one timeout left, but Coach King was screaming from the sideline not to use it. Matthew knew that he couldn't spike the ball, because it was fourth down. As soon as they got lined up, he took the snap and rolled to his right. He saw Dylan make a cut as he crossed to goal line. Matthew fired a bullet that hit him on the numbers for the Eagles touchdown.

The Benworth sideline was celebrating and the crowd was going insane. Tim tacked on the extra point. The bad news was that they still trailed by two points and there was only twenty-eight seconds left.

—

They lined up to try the onsides kick. Allegheny Hills put most of their return team just beyond midfield to try to recover it.

Tim squibbed the ball diagonally down the field. The Benworth players raced after it, while the Allegheny Hills players tried to block them out of the way. The second bounce went high into the air and came down into a sea of hands. Bodies were colliding as the ball bounced around. When it hit the ground, five or six players from each team dove for it all at once, creating a huge pile of players. A fight for the ball was taking place at the bottom of the pile.

Fans from both sides of the field were on their feet screaming. Players from both teams were signaling that they had recovered the ball. The officials were scrambling to see which team came up with it. They were trying to pull bodies off of the pile to see who had the ball at the bottom.

When they finally got everybody up, an Eagles player stood up and held the ball in the air. Cheers broke out from the Benworth side of the field, while groans could be heard from the Allegheny Hills side.

The onsides kick took five seconds off of the clock, so Matthew had only twenty-three seconds to get his team into field goal range.

—

In the huddle, Matthew felt a combination of anxious energy and excitement. He had played in a lot of games over the years, from pee wee league to middle school, but was never in a situation like this, with the game on the line.

He remembered the time he spent on the bench, wishing he would get the opportunity to play. Now he had it, and he didn't want to blow it. If he wanted to win the starting job away from Cody, he needed to come through in a big way.

Dylan grabbed him by the facemask and pulled him close. "You're doing great. I believe in you. Just keep doing what you've been doing all night, and you'll be fine."

Hunter added, "We can win this game."

Knowing that the team leaders had confidence in him had him so excited, he thought that he might leap out of his uniform. He took a deep breath and called the play.

—

The first pass was completed to Dylan at the thirty yard line, where he stepped out of bounds, stopping the clock with seventeen seconds left.

Matthew threw the next pass out of bounds when he didn't have an open receiver, taking the clock down to eleven seconds.

He knew that he had time for one more play before the field goal. He dropped back and saw that Dylan was double covered. He saw his tight end standing alone in the middle of the field. He tossed the ball his way, where he easily caught it. Turning up field, he was gang tackled at the seventeen yard line. Matthew called timeout with four seconds left on the clock.

—

Tim jogged onto the field to attempt a thirty-five yard field goal, easily within his range. He often made forty yard kicks in practice, so everyone on the team was confident that he would make it.

Before coming onto the field, he noticed the wind picking up, blowing across the field from left to right. He knew that he would have to take this into account when he made the kick.

He lined up, waited for the snap, and kicked the ball more to the left than he normally would have. At first, it looked like it would sail wide to the left, but as it got closer to the goal post, the wind changed the direction of the ball, splitting the uprights. The Eagles ran onto the field, jumping up and down with their arms in the air, but the celebration was short lived.

The officials were blowing their whistles and waving their arms over their heads. They quickly announced that Allegheny Hills had called timeout just before the ball was snapped.

Tim would have to do it again!

Boos filled the Benworth bleachers. They thought that they had won the game and didn't agree with the referee's ruling.

Tim was irritated, but confident that he could make the field goal a second time. He had judged the wind correctly and knew that he just needed to do exactly what he just did.

They lined up a second time. Once again, Tim kicked the ball to the left, but as he did, the wind died down. The ball wasn't changing direction! Every player, coach and fan held their breath as the ball flew through the air. As the ball came down, it clanged against the left upright and bounced back, landing in the end zone.

The kick was no good!

Tim dropped to his knees and covered his head with his hands. The Benworth fans stood watching in disbelief as the Allegheny Hills fans celebrated.

John ran onto the field to console Tim. When he got to him, he saw that Tim was crying. He tried to help him to his feet, but was shrugged off. John took a step back and patiently waited for him to get up on his own.

—

Matthew sat on the bench with his hands in his lap and his head hanging low. A few players came by and told him that he played well. He appreciated it, but was still disappointed about the loss.

After the teams lined up to shake hands, they headed back to the locker room. Matthew, Luke and Mark were walking about ten yards behind John and Tim.

As they got to the end of the field, Tim's father ran up to the fence, shouting obscenities at him. He was clearly intoxicated and Tim didn't look happy about it. He put his head down and kept walking, but it only made his dad angrier.

"YOU'RE WORTHLESS! IT'S YOUR FAULT THAT YOU LOST!"

Tim didn't acknowledge him.

"DON'T IGNORE ME!"

Tim kept walking with his head down.

"I SAID, DON'T IGNORE ME! YOU'D BETTER GET HOME IMMEDIATELY! I'LL BE WAITING FOR YOU!"

He continued shouting more profanity, but, by this time, they were in the locker room and couldn't hear him anymore.

—

Tim felt bad enough that he missed the field goal, but his dad embarrassing him put him over the edge. He broke into tears again. John put his arm around his shoulders, and this time, Tim didn't shake him off.

John asked, "Are you going to be alright?"

"Yeah. He gets like this when he's drunk. I'll be fine."

"You should come with us to Mario's. Matthew's buying."

"No. You heard my dad. I have to go home. Don't worry about me. I'll be okay."

"Do you want me to go to your house with you?"

"No. That would make him even more mad. If you don't mind, I'd like to be left alone."

John respected his wishes and went back to his own locker.

—

John looked at Matthew and said, "I'm worried about Tim. You saw how drunk his dad is."

"What should we do?"

"He wants to be alone. I want to go to his place with him, but he said that it would make things worse."

Matthew looked over to Tim, then back to John. "Let's pray for him."

They called Luke and Mark over and prayed for Tim's safety. When they were finished, John went back over to Tim and said, "Call me if you need anything."

Tim nodded, but didn't say anything. Tears were still streaming down his face.

John returned to his locker, shaking his head. He felt helpless. A sick feeling was growing in his stomach. He had a bad feeling that something terrible was going to happen that night.

CHAPTER 16

Matthew and John left the locker room after they finished changing and waited for Mark and Luke outside.

About fifty feet away, Matthew saw Coach King talking with Cody's father. He couldn't hear what they were saying, but Cody's dad was very animated, waving his arms around. Matthew assumed that he was upset about his son being pulled from the game. The coach was holding his hands out, trying to calm him down, but was having little success.

Matthew thought about getting closer to hear the argument but, just then, Cody's dad looked over and pointed right at him, stopping him in his tracks. Matthew looked away, not wanting to cause any trouble.

Mark and Luke came out and they started walking to Mario's. Matthew was silent most of the way, his mind on the game. They came so close. He couldn't help but wonder what would've happened if the coach had put him in the game sooner.

John didn't say anything, either. Matthew figured that he was probably worried about Tim, and that was why he was being quiet. A number of times, John took his cell phone out of his pocket and looked at it for a few seconds before putting it away again.

Luke and Mark joked around with each other, which seemed to irritate John. Matthew nudged him and said, "Don't worry. He'll be fine."

John looked at him as if he were insane. "How can you say that? We know that his dad hits him, and you saw how drunk and angry he is."

"We don't know anything for sure. He has some bruises that can't be explained, but we have no proof that his dad is responsible."

"I have a real bad feeling."

Matthew put his hand on his shoulder and said, "Try to relax and have fun tonight."

John nodded and kept walking.

Mario's was already packed when they arrived. The restaurant was loud with students laughing and carrying on. The noise from the video game area added to the chaotic scene.

They found Kylie and some of her friends, who already had a table saved. She motioned for Matthew to sit next to her, and he was eager to accommodate her request.

Scooting her chair closer to his, she said, "You played great tonight. That first field goal should have counted. I don't think that they called timeout before the ball was snapped."

"Unfortunately, the referee's don't agree, and their vote is the only one that counts."

"Are you going to be the starter now? I think that you proved tonight that you're the better quarterback."

"I guess that's up to the coach."

"Well, the coach is an idiot if he doesn't name you the new starter."

Matthew began to loosen up around Kylie. They continued to talk and got lost in the conversation. Time drifted by as he eventually forgot all about the game and had a fantastic time as he talked with the most beautiful girl he'd ever known.

—

Mark was surprised to see his sister, Madison, at the table, and even more surprised to see John sit next to her. They chatted as though they had been friends for years. Mark raised his eyebrows and wondered if there was something going on, but quickly discarded the idea. He reminded himself that Madison is two years older than John. A junior girl couldn't possibly be interested in a freshman boy, could she?

Luke challenged him to some video games and they got up to play them. His concentration repeatedly got diverted as he would look over his shoulder to see if John was still talking to his sister. He didn't know why it bothered him, but it did, nonetheless. The thought of one of his best and oldest friends dating his sister felt odd to him.

—

John had known Madison for a long time but, up until recently, he just viewed her as Mark's older sister. When they were younger, he would often spend the night at Mark's. For fun, they would play practical jokes on her, like setting her alarm clock to go off in the middle of the night, or stealing her diary so that they could find things about her to poke fun at. They were always finding clever ways to harass her.

When Madison was in her pre-teens, she was tall and scrawny. She kept her hair short and wore thick glasses.

Now, at the age of sixteen, the ugly duckling was turning into a swan. Her dark hair was now past her shoulders, full and wavy. She had traded in her glasses for contact lenses. She had a tiny button nose and full, rosy lips. Her body was developing nicely, adjusting to her tall frame.

John now looked at her in a new light. What used to be Mark's annoying older sister was now catching his eye every time he looked her way. They never got along while growing up but, now, as they sat next to each other, he found himself enjoying her company. He was actually considering the possibility of a romantic future between them.

The waitress brought the food to the table and they all dug in. They had a great time talking and making each other laugh. Before long, John had completely forgotten about Tim and what he might face at the hands of his father.

Once the food was gone, they all thanked Matthew for treating them. He sheepishly smiled and said, "It's alright. Kylie will be paying next week." Looking at her, he continued, "I want a rematch next Thursday night."

"You don't know when to quit, do you? It's your money."

Madison laughed and said, "My money's on Kylie. Any takers?"

John said, "Yeah. You're on!" Turning to Matthew, he said, "Don't let me down."

"No problem. I let her win last night."

With a big smile, Kylie said, "You wish!"

—

The night was winding down, so Luke called Pops to pick them up. As he pulled up in the minivan, John's cell phone rang.

He checked the caller ID and saw Tim's number. He flipped the phone open and said, "Tim, what's up?"

A concerned look came across John's face as he listened to what Tim told him. The other three looked intently as they waited for John to say something. Kylie walked out of the restaurant with a puzzled look, wondering what was going on.

John asked into his phone, "How bad are you hurt?" He paused for a few seconds and then asked, "Do you need to go to the hospital?"

They all started asking John questions at once, but he held his hand out, trying to quiet them so he could hear Tim. He finally said, "Stay put. We're on our way."

Pops got out of the minivan and asked, "What's wrong?"

"Tim's father beat him up tonight. He said that he's coughing up blood. We need to get him to the hospital!"

Pops looked enraged as he asked, "Where is his dad?"

"He's not sure. Tim said that he left a few minutes ago. He probably went to the bar."

"Everyone in the van. Let's get over there quickly."

Kylie asked, "Can I come with you?"

Pops answered, "Call your parents and have them come get you. We don't know where his dad is and it might not be safe."

Matthew grabbed her hand and said, "I'll call you later."

She gave him a tight hug and said, "Be careful."

He jumped in the minivan and Pops raced toward Tim's house.

While on the way, John asked, "Should we call for an ambulance?"

Pops replied, "We can probably get him to the hospital faster. We're only a couple minutes away."

Matthew asked, "What about the police? His dad should have to answer for this."

"One thing at a time. Let's get him some medical attention, then we'll worry about his father."

When they pulled up to Tim's driveway, he came out the front door and took a few steps before collapsing on the front lawn.

Pops jumped out and ran over to him. The kids were close behind. It was dark, but there was enough light coming from the porch light. They saw right away that there was bruising under his right eye and his lip was cut. Pops reached down to try to help him to the minivan, but when he touched him, Tim screamed.

"Where does it hurt?"

"Up and down my side. He kicked me there a bunch of times. I think my ribs are broken. It hurts just to breathe." He coughed a few times and blood trickled down his chin.

John got on the opposite side and he and Pops gently lifted him and helped him into the minivan. The rest piled in and they headed to the hospital.

As he backed out of the driveway, Pops asked, "Where is your father?"

Tim winced as he said, "He probably went to Floyd's Pub. That's where he usually goes on Friday nights."

"Has he done this before?"

Tim didn't respond. Pops continued, "Tim! You need to tell me if he's ever done this to you before."

"It's never been this bad before. He gets aggressive when he drinks. He's knocked me around a few times, but he never hurts me bad."

"Tell the doctors when we get there. What your father is doing is wrong and it needs to stop."

"I don't want him to get into trouble."

Pops sighed and said, "If you don't say something, I will."

"Please don't."

"Tim, the doctors are obligated to tell the authorities any time they suspect abuse. They're going to find out, one way or another. I recommend that you tell the truth, so this won't happen again. Your father needs help, so don't protect him."

Tim started crying. "He only does this when he's drunk."

"Then he needs to quit drinking."

Sitting next to him, John asked, "Did you lie about the bruise on your shoulder?"

He nodded. "He punched me because I spilled *Dr. Pepper* on the carpet."

"What about the bruises on your back a few weeks ago?"

"He was mad because I didn't wake him up in time for work. He was late and got docked some pay. It was my fault."

Pops said, "No! Do not take the blame for this. None of this is your fault. Your father is an adult and perfectly capable of waking himself up for work. It shouldn't be your responsibility."

Tim's sobs turned into wailing. "If I would have made the field goal, this never would have happened. He had a bet with a coworker and lost a lot of money."

Disgusted, Pops said, "That's no excuse."

They pulled up to the emergency room doors, where Luke jumped out to retrieve a wheelchair. They slowly helped Tim into it and wheeled him inside.

Pops went to the desk and explained the situation. A short time later, Tim was brought in for treatment.

The rest of them sat in the waiting room. It was getting late, so Pops insisted that they all call home and let their parents know where they were.

None of them wanted to go home until they knew whether or not Tim would be alright. Their parents agreed to let them stay, as long as Pops was there with them.

Matthew called Kylie and gave her a recap of what happened. She told him that she would call her friends to let them know, and to get everyone to pray for Tim.

—

John had a hard time sitting in one place. Time seemed to crawl by as he paced the waiting room. With Pops there, he couldn't talk to his friends about something that was troubling him.

Finally, Pops got up to use the restroom. John sat with the others and said, "Emmanuel is always telling us to pray. We prayed tonight for Tim's safety, and this happened anyway. I wish he was here now, so he could explain this to us."

Mark said, "I've been thinking the same thing."

Getting defensive, Matthew asked, "Are you trying to say that this is Emmanuel's fault?"

John answered, "No, of course not. This is Tim's father's fault. I'm just wondering how effective prayer really is. I really believed that when we prayed for him, that God would answer that prayer and prevent this from happening."

Luke said, "Pops always tells me that not all prayers are answered. It's up to God to decide and it's not our place to question that."

John scratched his head as he began pacing again. "It doesn't make sense to me."

Pops came back and they dropped the subject.

About two hours went by before the doctor finally got back to them. Pops ran up to him. "How is he?"

The others ran up behind to listen.

"He's going to be alright. Other than two broken ribs, there are no serious injuries. We're going to keep him overnight, just to be safe."

"Did he tell you how it happened?"

"Yes. We called Child Protective Services. The police are looking for his father."

"What happens from here?"

The doctor answered, "They're trying to locate other relatives that he can stay with."

Pops said, "He's welcome to stay with me until we can figure this out."

"I'm sure that won't be necessary. Hopefully by tomorrow morning, we'll find some relatives that we can release him to."

John asked, "Can we see him?"

"He's sleeping now. You guys should go home and get some rest."

—

Just before the bars closed for the night, two uniformed police officers went inside Floyd's Pub and found Rick Roman, Tim's father, sitting at the end of the bar. They read him his Miranda rights and arrested him on charges of child abuse. Rick didn't resist, but vehemently denied any wrongdoing. They put him in the back of their cruiser, and drove him to the county jail.

CHAPTER 17

Tim woke up Saturday morning in his hospital room. He didn't know where he was at first, but when he rolled over on to his side, the ache in his ribs flared up, reminding him of the beating he received the night before, at the hands of his father.

A nurse came in, gave him some pain medication, and served him a breakfast of fried eggs, bacon and toast. He devoured it as though he hadn't eaten in days.

When visiting hours began, Pops showed up with the kids. Tim sat up and greeted them with a smile. John shook his hand and asked him how he felt.

"The pills are helping, but my ribs are still pretty sore."

Pops pulled a chair up to the side of the bed. John and Luke occupied the other two chairs, while Matthew and Mark sat on the other bed, which was empty.

Pops laid his hand on Tim's arm and said, "I've been on the phone all morning, talking to a lot of people about your situation. I have quite a bit of news to tell you, and some of it won't be easy to hear. Are you ready?"

Tim nodded slowly, and Pops continued, "First of all, the police found your father in a bar last night, and they arrested him. At first, he denied everything, but after talking to a lawyer, he confessed. They're working on a plea bargain so he won't have to serve any prison time. He'll probably get probation, on the condition that he gets help for his drinking problem."

Tim let that sink in, then asked, "What kind of help are they talking about?"

"That will be up to the judge. It'll most likely be *Alcoholics Anonymous* meetings or possibly rehab. He'll probably have to attend anger management classes, as well."

Tears filled Tim's eyes. "I don't want anything bad to happen to him. I just don't want to get hurt anymore." He then broke down and started crying hard. He leaned forward with his hands covering his face.

John walked over and sat on the edge of the bed, putting his arm around his shoulder. "It's okay. Your dad is going to get the help that he needs."

"I know. I just hate the fact that it came to this. He was never like this before my mom died."

Pops waited a minute for Tim to compose himself, then took a deep breath before saying, "You're probably not going to like what I have to say next. The courts aren't going to allow you to stay with your father. Your grandparents, on your mother's side, are driving in from Philadelphia tomorrow. They're taking you back and you're going to stay with them. I talked to them this morning and they're very angry with your father."

Pops looked surprised as Tim's face lit up. "I'm looking forward to seeing them. I haven't seen them since the funeral. I was supposed to visit them for a few weeks every summer, but my dad always changed his mind at the last minute. They've never gotten along with my dad."

"The hospital is releasing you, and your grandparents have given permission for you to stay with me until they get here."

John added, "We've decided to keep you company today." He showed him a plastic bag that he had brought with him and pulled out a soccer video game. "We stopped on the way and bought this. When we get back to Pops' house, we'll play this for a while."

Tim smiled and started to feel warm inside. He really appreciated the help that he was receiving. "Thanks guys. That's awesome."

Pops asked, "Did you tell the doctors everything last night?"

"Yeah. It wasn't easy, but the more I thought about it, the more I knew that I had to do it. It's gotten worse with time, and I got really scared that the next time would be real bad. I don't want there to be a next time."

"That's good. This has gone on long enough."

A voice came from the door. "Good morning."

Everyone looked toward the sound of the voice and saw Pastor Alex standing there. "Matthew's parents called me this morning and told me what happened."

John stood up and allowed the pastor to come to the side of the bed. He asked, "How are you feeling?"

"I've been better. The physical pain isn't nearly as bad as the sick feeling that I have in the pit of my stomach."

"I know that this must be difficult. Even though your father isn't a member of the church, I'm feeling compelled to visit him in the county jail. Is there anything that you'd like me to ask him?"

"Tell him that I forgive him."

"I will. Does your dad know the Lord?"

Tim shook his head. "I don't think so. He never went to church, even when my mom was alive. He doesn't know that I've been attending your church. It'll probably be a surprise to him."

"You know him better than me. Do you think he'll be open to talking about God?"

"As long as he's sobered up from last night. He turns into a different person when he's drunk. He's a nice guy when he's not drinking."

Pastor Alex asked him, "Would you mind telling me a little history of what led up to this? I'd like to have some background before I talk to him. Was he always a heavy drinker?"

"I remember him drinking from time to time as I grew up. He might have a beer or two while watching the Steelers or Penguins, but he never went to bars until after my mom died."

"I imagine that he took your mother's death pretty hard."

"I think that he blames himself." He felt himself getting choked up as he recalled the events. "There was a real bad snow storm that night. She was visiting a friend in Youngstown and called to tell him that she was going to spend the night there. The roads were bad, so she didn't want to drive. He insisted that she come home anyway. Her accident happened on the turnpike while driving home."

"The guilt must be eating him up inside."

Tim started crying again. "Sometimes I blame him, too. If he would've just agreed to let her stay overnight, she'd still be alive today."

"We can't change the past. You said that you forgive him for hitting you. Maybe you can forgive him for this, too."

"I know I should, but it's hard."

"Forgiveness is never easy, but it's very freeing. If you can find it in your heart to do so, I guarantee that you'll feel better about it."

"I'll try."

"Alright. Let's move on if we can. How did the abuse start?"

"For the first few months after the funeral, he didn't say much. He would come home from work and drink until he passed out. After a while, he picked himself up enough to start going out. Before long, he was going to the bars every night. There were some days when he wouldn't speak to me at all. He wouldn't even bother to say goodbye when he left."

Pastor Alex shook his head and asked, "Did you try talking to him?"

"Sometimes, but it usually led to him being critical of everything I did, so I stopped talking to him, too. He would make me feel so insignificant."

"What was he critical of?"

"Everything. Pretty much all of the house and yard work became my responsibility, but my work was never good enough for him. The dishes were never clean enough. The bushes were never trimmed properly. His steak was never cooked to his liking. It went on and on. No matter how hard I tried to please him, it was never good enough."

"So, all of the household chores fell on your shoulders after your mom died?"

"I was already doing the outside stuff. That started when I was ten or eleven. My mom always did the inside work. After she died, he told me that I would have to do it, because he didn't have time."

"Tell me about the first time that he hit you."

"I came home from school one day and he was sitting in his chair, drinking and watching TV. He usually works until 5:00, so I was surprised to see him. When I asked why he wasn't at work, he told me that he was sick and came home early. I asked him why he was drinking if he was sick and he backhanded me across the face. He said something about respecting him and that I better never question him again."

"So, he only struck you once that first time?"

"Yeah. It got worse, later. It was only when he was drunk. Now, he's drunk almost all of the time."

Pastor Alex sighed and said, "Hopefully, we've seen the last of it. I'm going to visit him now."

Tim looked longingly at the pastor. "Please understand that it's a combination of the alcohol and how much he misses my mom. He was never mean before she died."

"I have a lot of experience dealing with people grieving and suffering from addiction. I'm very compassionate to those people. I'm just going to encourage him to get the help that he needs. Who knows? When it's all said and done, maybe he'll give his life to Christ. I've seen it happen before."

Tim smiled from ear to ear and said, "That would be awesome."

Pastor Alex turned to the other kids and asked, "Have you guys been staying out of the woods?"

Matthew responded, "Yeah. We haven't gone in there."

John added, "There's been so much going on that we haven't really even thought about it. We have much more important things happening right here."

Looking confused, Tim asked, "What's in the woods?"

Pastor Alex put his hand on his shoulder and said, "Don't worry about it. It's not important. You just concentrate on healing from these injuries. When are you getting out of here?"

"Today. It should be soon."

Pops said, "We're waiting for the doctor to release him."

"That's good. Take care of yourself in Philly." He shook hands with everybody and left to go visit Tim's father.

Shortly after, Tim was released from the hospital. They spent the remainder of the day playing the soccer video game and doing their best to cheer Tim up.

—

After leaving the hospital, Pastor Alex drove over to the county jail. He was led to a chair in front of a glass partition with a phone hanging from the wall. There was an identical chair and phone on the other side of the glass.

He waited patiently for about ten minutes, then Rick Roman was led in by a guard. He was dressed in an orange jumpsuit. His straight brown hair was sticking up in places and his face was covered with razor stubble. He looked like he had just woken up.

Rick sat in the chair and picked up the phone with a bewildered look on his face. "Do I know you?"

"No. My name is Alex Ezra. I'm the lead pastor at Fellowship Trinity Church in Benworth."

"I haven't seen the inside of a church since my wife's funeral. Before that, my wedding. Why are you here?"

"I just talked to your son at the hospital. I promised him that I would come talk to you."

"How do you know my son?"

"I don't know him well. Some of his friends attend my church and they brought him with them this past Sunday. I found out what happened this morning, so I paid him a visit. He told me some disturbing things."

Rick lowered his head. "I don't know what he's told you, but I've done nothing wrong."

"He said that you've been abusing him for years."

"That's a lie."

"Then why did you confess?"

A tear ran down the right side of his face, which he wiped with the back of his hand. He sniffed loudly and said, "I was just following my lawyer's advice. He told me that I won't have to serve any jail time if I plead guilty to a lesser charge."

"Well, if you've done nothing wrong, why plead guilty?"

Rick peered through the glass with a sinister look on his face. "I already told you. It was my lawyer's idea. You're starting to annoy me and it's not helping my hangover."

"Are you telling me that you've never hit your son?"

"I may have gotten physical with him a few times, but it wasn't abuse. My old man treated me a lot worse when I was his age."

"He just spent the night in the hospital. That's a lot more than getting physical. You have a problem and it needs to be addressed."

"Why do you care?"

Pastor Alex raised his voice a little as he responded, "Because crimes against kids make me sick. What you're doing to Tim disgusts me and I want to see it stop."

Rick stood up and screamed, "You preacher types are all the same. Do you think that because you're on that side of the glass that you can look down on me?"

"Relax. I'm not here to cause problems. I only want to help."

"Help with what?"

"For starters, your drinking. Tim told me that you weren't always a heavy drinker, that it didn't start until after your wife died. Is that true?"

Rick sat back down, a calm demeanor overtaking him. "Yeah. I needed something to numb the pain. She was everything to me. I never knew how much I depended on her until she was gone."

"You know that alcohol is a depressant, right? Although you may think it's helping, it's actually making you feel worse."

Rick leaned back in his chair and slouched. "I didn't know what else to do."

"The judge is most likely going to order you to attend *Alcoholics Anonymous* meetings. We also have a program at the church called *Set Free*. It's a program for any kind of addiction. I've seen a lot of people get delivered from all kinds of problems in their lives. Even though you're not a member of our church, you're welcome to attend."

"I'm not addicted to anything. Sure, I like to have a few drinks after work, but I'm not an alcoholic. I'll attend those meetings if the judge tells me to, but it's not going to change anything."

"What about gambling? Tim said that you had a bet on his high school game. Is this another area in which you need help?"

"I'll admit that I have a bookie, but I usually only bet on the Steelers. Sometimes on the Monday night game, just to make it interesting. Just casual betting. It's not a problem."

"You had a large bet on a high school football game. That's not casual betting. Sounds like it could be a problem to me."

Rick rubbed his chin and looked up. "I know that from your standpoint, it looks pretty bad, but I don't need help."

"Are you aware that they're not going to allow Tim to stay with you?"

He nodded and said, "My lawyer told me. Where is he going to stay?"

"Your wife's parents are coming to get him. He's going to live with them in Philadelphia for a while."

"I'm sure that they're loving this."

"Tim told me that you don't get along with them. Why not?"

"They were never happy about my wife marrying me. Before she met me, she was dating a doctor in Philly. When they broke up, she came to visit a friend here in Pittsburgh. I met her at the stadium, watching the Pirates play. We hit it off and she decided to move here. We got married a few months later. Her parents wanted her to get back together with the doctor and they never approved of me. I took it personally and always held it against them."

"Why didn't they approve of you?"

"They're big on religion. They wanted their daughter to marry a Christian man."

"What about the times that Tim was supposed to visit them? He said that you always cancelled those trips at the last minute."

"They've treated me like a second class citizen since the first time I met them. This was my way of paying them back."

"Denying them a chance to see their grandson seems kind of harsh."

"If you'd heard some of the things they said to me at the funeral, you'd understand. With you being a holy man and all, I won't say them out loud. Let's just say that they weren't very Christian like."

"Keep in mind that they were grieving, too. You lost your wife, but they lost their daughter. They were hurting just as bad. I'm sure that they didn't really mean what they said."

"Oh, yes they did. To this day, they still blame me for her death. When they found out that I insisted that she come home on the night of her accident, they went ballistic. They kept saying that I killed her. The pain and guilt that I was feeling was horrible, and they had to add to it with all of the cruel things that they said to me. I will never forget the way that they treated me, and I will never forget the things that they said to me at the funeral."

"Are you okay with Tim staying with them?"

Rick laughed out loud. "Are you kidding me? I can't stand those self righteous Jesus freaks! But I guess there's nothing that I can do about it."

"Are you worried about it?"

"Not worried. I know that they'll be kind to him, but I'm pretty sure that they'll try to turn him against me. Who knows what kind of lies they're planning to tell him?"

Feeling like he needed to change the subject, Alex said, "Tim said that you're very critical of the work he does around the house. He says that nothing is ever good enough for you."

"I'm preparing him for the real world. When he joins the working force, he needs to be ready for what his bosses will expect from him."

"Now that Tim is going to Philadelphia, you'll be living alone. Do you think you can handle that?"

"I don't have a choice."

"You'll probably be released after the hearing on Monday. What do you plan to do?"

"I'm not sure. I'm going to have to make some adjustments."

"You said that you haven't been inside a church since the funeral. Why is that? Do you believe in God?"

"I guess I do. It's not something that I think about very often."

"Has anyone ever talked to you about Jesus?"

"My wife tried a few times. I was never interested. I feel like religion has too many restrictions. I don't think that there's anything wrong with my lifestyle."

"It's not about restrictions. It's about a personal relationship with Christ."

"That's what she said, but it's not for me."

"Do you know that Jesus died for you?"

"I've heard all this before. I don't know what to think about it."

"Well, I'm not going to sit here and try to convince you of anything, but I would like to invite you to attend my church."

"Maybe. I'll give it some thought, but no promises."

"I hope to see you there. You can call me if you ever want to talk. I'll leave my business card with your attorney. I'm going to leave now, but I want to tell you one last thing. The best way to turn your life around is to give your life to God. I've seen it happen more times than I could count."

"Look, I'm not perfect, but things are not as bad as you seem to think."

Pastor Alex smiled and said, "Take care and God bless. I'll be in touch."

He left the jail and headed for home. As he drove, he thought about how much he dreaded this part of being a pastor. He hated talking to people about their problems, but it was very rewarding when he saw positive results.

He wasn't encouraged by his talk with Rick. As he waited at a traffic light, he bowed his head and said a prayer for Rick and Tim Roman. When he finished, he looked to the street corner. He saw a man with long brown hair and a beard, dressed in a gray hoodie and blue jeans. The man was smiling at him. After nodding to Alex, he turned around and walked away, disappearing behind a building.

Pastor Alex wasn't sure why, but he looked very familiar to him.

Chapter 18

Arriving at church earlier than usual, Matthew and David sat on the curb outside the youth center, waiting for Zeke to get there and unlock the doors. They talked quietly while watching people drive up for Sunday service.

Matthew's attention was diverted when he saw Coach King and Cody's father talking in the parking lot. It was the first time that he'd seen Cody's dad at church. He wondered if he was there to attend church or just to talk to the coach.

Their conversation appeared to be getting heated, which drew a small crowd. Cody's father yelled out to them, "Mind your own business!"

Coach King held his hands out to let everyone know that it was under control. The others kept their distance, but continued watching.

Not being able to hear what was being said, Matthew stood up and took a few steps toward them. David swiftly stepped up to prevent him from getting too close. They both watched intently, but were careful not to be conspicuous about it.

The coach was trying to calm him down as they talked. After a couple minutes, Coach King said something that seemed to satisfy Cody's dad. They shook hands and went their separate ways. Cody's father returned to his car and drove off.

David asked, "You know what that was about, don't you?"

"Yeah. They were arguing after the game Friday night, too."

"Prepare yourself. There's a good chance that Cody will be named the starter again for the next game. His dad pulls a lot of weight at the school. He's used to getting his way and won't rest until he does."

Matthew shrugged his shoulders and acted like he didn't care. On the inside, it was bothering him that the coach would even consider starting

Cody instead of him, especially after the past Friday night's results. He knew the decision was out of his hands and tried to put it out of his mind.

The thought left his mind when Pops pulled up and dropped Luke and Tim off. They small talked for a bit.

Luke was explaining to Tim that all of the classes that day would be combined. One Sunday per month, they would put all the classes together and meet in the large youth group room. The teachers rotated their schedule, allowing the rest to take a week off. Zeke was teaching them this month.

Matthew checked his watch and wondered where Zeke was. He gazed around and stopped short. He wasn't sure, but he thought he saw Emmanuel walk into the sanctuary. Were his eyes playing tricks on him? He considered running over to the other building to see if it really was him, but before he could, Zeke appeared and unlocked the door. Everyone followed him inside and took their seats. Matthew joked around with Luke and Tim while they waited for class to begin.

Kylie walked in a few minutes later and smiled at Matthew, making his heart melt. He had to keep reminding himself what Emmanuel had said about just being her friend. She came over to him and greeted him with a hug, then sat in the seat next to him. Matthew wasn't sure if it was his imagination or not, but Kylie's hugs seemed to be getting longer each time. He certainly wasn't upset about this.

At the top of the hour, Zeke started the class. "Open your bibles to Galatians, chapter five. Today, we're going to talk about the fruit of the Spirit." He paused, giving the students time to find the right page, then continued, "Let's look at verses twenty-two and twenty-three. 'But the fruit of the Spirit is love, joy, peace, patience, kindness, goodness, faithfulness, gentleness and self-control. Against such things, there is no law.'"

He allowed this to sink in, then added, "I want to focus on joy, today. You're at an age when the pressures of life can bring you down. What are some of the problems that teens deal with?"

Hands went up and the responses were vast. Drinking, drugs, grades, whether or not to have sex, trying to fit in, dealing with bullies, peer pressure, and the list went on and on.

Zeke asked, "How do we keep our joy while dealing with these things?"

No one raised their hand. Zeke flipped the pages of his bible, found what he was looking for, and read aloud, "John 16:22 says, 'So with you:

Now is your time of grief, but I will see you again and you will rejoice, and no one will take away your joy.'" He closed his bible, took off his glasses, and stood up to address the class. "Do you know what that means? Jesus said that to his disciples. He was telling us that the world is going to throw a lot of things our way, and we're going to experience grief and sorrow in our lives. However, when we accept Jesus as our savior, we receive joy that can never be taken away from us. His resurrection changed things forever, bringing us joy that will overcome the world."

Matthew looked over to Tim and saw tears in his eyes. He quickly looked away so he wouldn't embarrass him. He felt so much compassion for him. He couldn't imagine how hard this must be on him.

Zeke went on, "What are some of the things we can do to hold on to our joy when we're going through difficult times?"

At first, no one responded, then David slowly raised his hand and Zeke called on him. "Thanks to a suggestion from Pastor Alex, I've been reading my bible everyday. It's really helped me to come to terms with my injury. I may never play football again, but that's fine. I believe that God has better plans for me."

Zeke just stood there with an amazed look on his face. A few seconds later, he snapped out of it and said, "Wow! That's awesome. Is there a specific scripture that helped you?"

"I came across Romans 8:28, and it jumped off the page."

"Would you read it for us?"

David fanned through his bible and found it. He cleared his throat and recited, "And we know that in all things God works for the good of those who love him, who have been called according to his purpose."

Zeke rubbed his chin and asked, "How did that help you?"

"Well, I was really bummed out. I felt like my whole future had been taken from me. When I read that scripture, two things came to my mind. First, that good things can come from something that initially appears to be bad and, second, that God's purpose can be different from my own. After reading this, I came to believe this injury happened because I was going down the wrong road and God wanted to put me on the right path."

"Do you think that you now know what the right path for your life is?"

"I think so. In fact, I'm going to talk to Pastor Alex about some things after service. I have some ideas about my future that I'd like to discuss with him."

"Great! It sounds like reading God's Word has really touched your life in a positive way. Is anyone else reading the bible everyday?"

Matthew and Kylie raised their hands simultaneously. They looked at each other with surprise.

Zeke asked, "Matthew, were you inspired to do this by your brother?"

"No. I started because a good friend recommended it." He was careful not to mention Emmanuel by name.

"That's good. What about you, Kylie?"

She answered, "My dad got me started a few years ago. I've read the whole thing and now I'm going through it a second time."

"That's amazing! For someone your age to have read it once is a great accomplishment, but you're reading it a second time. Keep it up!"

Zeke went on with the lesson while Kylie blushed a little.

Matthew whispered to her, "I had no idea. I've got some catching up to do."

She smiled and reached over to give his hand a quick squeeze, then let go.

When the class was dismissed, the kids filed out into the parking lot. Some went to the sanctuary to find their parents, while others broke into groups and talked.

Matthew, Kylie and Luke were talking when Zeke came up to them. "I think it's cool that you guys are reading the bible. Have you ever considered starting a small group to study it together? I belong to a group that meets at a friend's house on Saturday nights. It's helped a lot. I can't say enough good things about it."

Kylie replied, "I had a group in New York. I was hoping to find one here."

Zeke asked, "Why don't you guys start one? If you could find an adult who was willing to lead it, I'm sure it would be a huge blessing for all of you."

Just then, Pops walked up. "I overheard what you were talking about. I'd be happy to lead it for you. I've been leading an adult group for years, so I know what it entails."

Matthew said, "That would be perfect." He turned to Kylie and added, "You invite some of your friends and I'll invite some of mine."

Kylie's face lit up. "When should we start?"

Pops thought about it and said, "Mondays work for me."

Matthew smiled and said, "Cool! Spread the word. Tomorrow is kind of short notice, so why don't we start next week?"

Pops nodded and turned to Luke. "Where's Tim?"

He pointed toward the parking lot and they walked over to where he was talking to John. Pops asked him, "Are you ready to go?"

"Give me one minute."

Matthew followed as Tim went over to David and told him, "I really appreciate what you shared in there today. Along with what Zeke said, I heard a lot of things that I needed to hear. Thank you."

David shook his hand and said, "You're going to come out of this just fine."

—

David said goodbye to his friends and headed to the sanctuary so he could talk to Pastor Alex. He went inside and took a seat in the front row. He leaned his crutches against the chair next to him and waited for the pastor to finish talking to the other congregates.

His father came over and asked him, "Are you ready to leave?"

"You guys go on ahead. I'll catch a ride with Jocelyn. I want to stay and talk to the pastor about something."

"Are you alright?"

"Yeah. I just want his advice on something. It's nothing to worry about."

His dad nodded and left to take his wife and Matthew home.

When Pastor Alex finished talking and praying with the people who were waiting in line, he saw David sitting there and went over to him. "David, how are you today?"

"I'm good. I was hoping to discuss something with you."

Pastor Alex sat in the chair next to him and said, "Of course. What's on your mind?"

"First of all, I'd like to thank you for coming over to my house and talking to me. At the time, I didn't want to hear anything from anybody, but I learned a lot that night."

"Like what?"

"For one thing, there's more to life than football. Don't get me wrong. I'm still upset about not being able to play. It eats me up inside every Friday night, having to watch the games from the sidelines, but I know that God has other plans for me."

Alex leaned back in his chair and asked, "Do you think you know what those plans are?"

"I think God is calling me to be a pastor."

Pastor Alex gave him a stern look. "Our conversation was less than two weeks ago. You haven't had a lot of time to think about this."

"I know. I've been reading the bible that you gave me. I'm really enjoying the gospels. The more I read about Jesus, the more I want to learn about him. I want to share what I learn with others, and the best way to do that would be to become a pastor."

"There are other ways to share the gospel. There's a lot more to being a pastor than just preaching from the pulpit. I don't think that you have any idea how demanding this job can be."

David looked down and stared at the floor for a moment, then looked up and said, "I'm not afraid of hard work."

"It's not the work that I'm talking about. It's a very thankless job. This doesn't apply to everyone in the church, but a lot of people expect me to pay exclusive attention to their problem. They expect me to solve their marriage problems. They expect me to find jobs for them. They expect me to find roommates for them. Some of them even want money from the church. It never ends and, when I can't deliver to their satisfaction, they blame me."

"The way that you talked about it last week, I wouldn't have ever guessed that you felt this way."

"Don't think for a second that I regret my decision. I love being a pastor. I just want you to know what you have in store for yourself if you go through with this. You probably think that this is a glamorous job because I stand in front of hundreds of people every week delivering a message. That is my favorite part of what I do, but it's just the beginning. I'm doing administrative work all week long, as well as helping people with their problems. I have to be available to people twenty-four hours a day. Sometimes, it's people who don't even attend our church. Yesterday, I spent time talking to Tim at the hospital and his dad at the jail. I would much rather have spent my Saturday watching college football."

"I still think I want to do it."

"What about college?"

"I'm still going to go to college, but I think it would be awesome to have a career that is also a ministry."

"There's nothing wrong with that. Just think about what I've told you and pray about it. You still have the rest of your senior year ahead of you. Enjoy it and study hard. Attend college and see where the Lord leads you."

David grabbed his crutches and stood up. He looked back at the pastor and asked, "After you got hurt, did you miss playing football?"

"I still miss it. Some of my favorite memories took place on the football field. Over time, I was able to accept the situation and make my peace with it. The desire to play will probably always be there."

"That's what I was afraid of."

Pastor Alex laughed out loud. "It gets easier as time goes on. When I said that I'm available twenty-four hours a day, I meant it. Call me if you need to talk."

They shook hands and David hobbled off to find Jocelyn. They spent the rest of the day together, watching football during the afternoon and then going to the movies.

When he got home that night, he went into his bedroom for some privacy and prayed. He asked God to guide him and help him to make the right decisions regarding his career choice.

His last thought before falling asleep was that Pastor David Peters had a nice ring to it.

CHAPTER 19

Rick Roman sat in the courtroom, waiting patiently for his name to be called. It was late Monday morning and he had just spent the weekend in jail. He'd been sitting there for a couple of hours already and just wanted to get this over with so he could go to the bar.

While others who had also been arrested over the weekend were appearing before the judge, Rick thought about what had happened over the last few years. How did it come to this?

Since his wife's death, his life had spun out of control. Before she died, he was content with his life. Now, he felt like his whole life was crashing down around him.

Since his arrest late Friday night, he'd had a lot of time to think about what he needed to do to get his life in order. With the exception of his conversations with his attorney, and then with Pastor Alex, Saturday was a bit of a blur. He spent most of the day wishing that his hangover would go away. His head cleared a little on Sunday, giving him the chance to give a lot of thought about what he wanted to do with his life.

The thought of giving up alcohol scared him. It was what he relied on when things got tough. The *A.A.* meetings, that the judge was likely to order him to attend, didn't bother him. He knew that he could endure them and go through the motions.

He'd thought about quitting drinking a few times over the last year or so, but never made it more than a few days before giving in and taking another drink. Deep down, he knew that he had a drinking problem, but lacked the self-control to stop on his own.

He felt torn. A part of him wanted to quit, and another wanted nothing more than to have another beer. It was a constant battle going on inside his mind.

He was startled when he heard his name called. He stood up quickly and walked forward to face the judge. His attorney strolled up beside him.

Rick tried to remember what he and his lawyer had talked about Saturday morning, but just like a lot of things in his life, it was all a little hazy. He was even having a hard time recalling his lawyer's name. Lee, or was it Leon? It wasn't important. After this was over, he was hoping to never see him again, or any other attorney, for that matter.

The attorney was tall and thin, with wavy gray hair. Rick guessed his age to be somewhere around sixty. His deep, booming voice resonated throughout the courtroom.

As the judge and his attorney talked back and forth, Rick wasn't really listening. He already knew what the result of his plea agreement necessitated. He just wanted to get out of there so he could go to the bar and have a drink.

He began paying attention when the judge started handing down his ruling. "I am sentencing you to one year of probation. I am also ordering you to attend an anger management program as well as thirty *Alcoholics Anonymous* meetings."

His lawyer spoke up, "Your Honor, a local pastor recommended a program that is offered at his church called *Set Free*. Would that be acceptable in place of *A.A.*?"

"I'll accept that."

The judge slammed his gavel and went on to the next case.

Rick and his attorney left the courthouse. Lee, or Leon, Rick still wasn't sure of his name and was too embarrassed to ask, gave him a ride back to his car, which was still at Floyd's Pub.

The first few minutes of the ride went by quietly. Rick broke the silence by saying, "Thanks for getting me off the hook."

"You were lucky this time. Make sure that you follow the judge's instructions. Don't miss any appointments with your probation officer and go to all the meetings. Stay out of the bars, and most importantly, don't hit your son again."

Rick scratched his head. "Well, he's going to be in Philadelphia, so I guess I won't have the chance." Anger overcame him as he thought about his son living hundreds of miles away with people he didn't even like.

They pulled into the parking lot of Floyd's Pub. They shook hands as Rick said, "Nothing personal, but I hope I never see you again."

His attorney laughed and said, "Me too." He reached into his suit jacket pocket and pulled out a business card. "The pastor that you met the other day wanted me to give this to you."

Rick took the card and put it in his back pocket. He thought to himself that he would throw it away later, but didn't want to do it in front of his lawyer.

His attorney continued, "He seems like a good guy. Maybe you should call him about the *Set Free* meetings."

"I'll keep that in mind."

He exited the car and closed the door. He got into his own car but didn't start the ignition. He had no intention of leaving yet. As soon as his attorney left the parking lot, he got out of his car and started walking toward the bar.

As he got close to the entrance, he noticed a man leaning against the wall, a few feet away from the door. The man was wearing a gray hoodie and jeans. He had long brown hair and a beard. Rick eyed him up and down as he approached. He'd never seen him before and wondered why he was standing outside the bar by himself.

When Rick was a few feet away from the door, the man calmly said, "The bar is closed."

Rick tried to open the door, but it was locked. He looked at his watch and said, "They open at noon. It's almost two o'clock."

The man just shrugged his shoulders.

Rick pressed his ear against the door and said, "I can hear people inside. There's music playing on the jukebox. Why is the door locked?" He proceeded to knock on the door. When nobody opened it, he started pounding his fist and shouting out, "Open up!"

"I told you that they're closed."

Rick scowled at him. "Then why are there people inside?"

The man sighed and said, "You don't want to go in there."

Rick could feel anger burning up inside of him. "What do you know about what I want?"

"You'd be surprised by how much I know."

"Well, let me tell you something. You don't know anything about me."

"Did you learn anything while spending the weekend in jail?"

Rick took a step toward him, closing the gap. "How did you know that I was in jail?"

"Like I said, you'd be surprised by how much I know."

"I'm in no mood to play games. Do you want to tell me who you are and how you know me?"

"My friends call me Emmanuel." The man smiled and started to walk to the parking lot, with Rick following a step behind. When they reached Rick's car, Emmanuel turned around and asked, "Why do you want to go into the bar so bad?"

"I have a lot going on, and a drink would help me calm my nerves."

"There's a lot better ways to calm your nerves than drinking."

"Like what?"

"Have you ever tried praying?"

Rick scoffed and said, "That might work for the holy rollers out there, but it won't work for me."

"You didn't answer my question. Have you ever tried it?"

"No."

"Then how can you be so quick to dismiss it."

Rick felt a little flustered as he responded, "I guess I don't know for sure, but I do know that drinking works."

"Does it?"

"Of course!"

"It seems to me like it's just the opposite. How many fights have you gotten into at this very bar?"

"Those weren't my fault."

"How about all the times that you hit your son?"

"That's been blown way out of proportion."

Emmanuel folded his arms across his chest and leaned against the car. "Who are you trying to convince? Me, or yourself?"

Rick stood there, dumbfounded.

Before he could answer, a black SUV rolled into the parking lot and pulled into the spot next to Rick's car. A man that Rick knew as Louie, a regular at Floyd's Pub, stepped out. Louie gave Rick a nod of recognition, then looked at Emmanuel suspiciously.

Rick said to Louie, "The bar is closed."

Louie looked back, gave him a puzzled look, and walked to the entrance. He quietly opened the door and disappeared inside.

Rick's eyes lit up as he said, "Oh good! It's open." He started walking fast, calling back to Emmanuel, "If you want to continue this conversation, you're going to have to buy me a drink."

When he got to the door, he pulled on the handle, but it wouldn't budge. He tried a few more times without success. "What's going on?"

Emmanuel walked up behind him and said, "I told you, the bar is closed."

"Then how did Louie get inside? Listen, you can hear people and music."

"If you go in there and drink, you're only going to feel worse. Alcohol has a violent affect on you. If you want to turn your life around, you need to quit drinking."

Rick started pacing around the parking lot with his hands on his head. "I don't know what else to do?"

"The meetings that the judge ordered you to attend will be a good start. You could also go talk to the pastor that came to visit you in jail."

"I'm still trying to figure out why that guy came to visit me. He doesn't even know me. Why does he care?"

Emmanuel jammed his hands into his pockets, leaned back against the wall, and said, "It's because he doesn't want to see your son get hurt anymore, and quite frankly, I don't either."

Rick was feeling totally confused as he glared at Emmanuel. "Who are you and how do you know so much about me?"

Emmanuel smiled at him and said, "Let's just say that I'm someone who cares and loves you."

"How can you know and love me when we've never even met before?"

"I've always known you."

Rick was taken aback. "Are you expecting me to believe that you're God, or something?"

"I'm telling you the truth. If you want to salvage your relationship with Tim, you're going to have to quit drinking. This kind of behavior is something that can be passed down from generation to generation. You can put an end to that, right now."

"I just want to have one drink."

"One drink will not satisfy you. It'll only make you want more."

Rick lowered his head and said, "I know."

"Help is available if you're willing to accept it. The choice is up to you."

For the next twenty seconds, Rick stood still, staring at Emmanuel. They eventually smiled at each other, prompting Rick to say, "This is so weird. I just met you a few minutes ago, yet I feel like I can trust you. I don't think I've ever trusted anyone other than my wife."

"Tell me something. What do you want more than anything?"

"I want my wife back. Since she died, I have had this void in my life that I can't seem to fill, no matter what I do."

Emmanuel nodded. "I know that you miss her. How have you tried to fill the void?"

"I don't know. I guess I kept thinking that the end of my pain would be found at the bottom of a beer bottle. I'm slowly learning that it's not. I have to admit that I have no idea how to fill that void."

"God is the only one who can fill it."

"That sounds like something my wife would've said."

"Have you ever thought about what she would think about how you've lived your life since she died?"

Rick paused before responding, "Not really, but now that I think about it, she'd probably be disappointed. Especially the way that I've treated my son."

"It's not too late to start doing the right thing. Your son still loves you. He's already forgiven you."

"I don't know why. I can't even forgive myself."

"Why not?"

"Because this whole thing is my fault. My wife died because I insisted that she come home on a night when the roads were bad. If I had let her spend the night at her friend's house, she would still be alive today. Why did I have to be such a jerk?"

"Your wife died in a tragic accident. You can't spend the rest of your life blaming yourself."

"How can I not blame myself? I was the one who told her to drive in a blizzard. It was my selfish decision that caused her death."

"Do you realize that this is why you're having a hard time getting over the pain?"

"So many people have told me that time will heal these wounds, but it's been four years and the pain is still there. It hurts just as much today as it did the day that I got the news."

"God can heal your pain, but you have to allow Him to."

"I still don't understand how you know so much about me. Are you God?"

"The next chance you get, I want you to get a bible and read Isaiah 7:14. I think that it'll help you to understand."

Emmanuel slowly walked up to him and put his arms around him. At first, Rick kept his arms by his side then, after a few seconds, lightly returned the hug.

Emmanuel whispered in his ear, "Maybe you should take that card out of your back pocket and call Pastor Alex."

Rick started weeping as they broke the hug. He watched silently as Emmanuel turned around and walked around the corner of the building.

He wasn't sure what just happened. It almost seemed like a dream. Could giving his life to God really end his pain?

He took the business card out of his pocket and looked at it for a minute or so. He looked back and forth between the entrance to the bar and the card. Finally, he walked back to the car and took his cell phone out. He dialed the number on the card and thought to himself that he was making the right decision.

—

Pastor Alex was feeling anxious. It had been about fifteen minutes since he'd received a phone call from Rick Roman, who was on his way to visit him.

Alex was surprised to hear from him. The conversation they'd had two days earlier hadn't gone well. He left the county jail feeling as though he'd failed to accomplish anything. He wondered why Rick wanted to see him. What had changed since Saturday afternoon?

He glanced out of his office window and saw Rick getting out of his car. He looked much better than he had on Saturday. His tight white t-shirt revealed an impressive physique. Despite his problems, he'd managed to keep his body in pretty good shape.

Rick looked around and appeared to be unsure of where to go. Alex swiftly got up and met him in the parking lot. They shook hands and Alex led him back to his office.

As Alex sat in the chair behind his desk, he asked, "What can I do for you?"

Rick slowly sat in one of the two seats in front of the desk and said, "I want to change my life, but I have no idea how."

Alex dipped his head. "If you don't mind me asking, what changed between the last time we spoke and now? You didn't seem to want my help a couple days ago."

"I've had a really crazy day. If I told you what just happened to me, you probably wouldn't believe it."

"Try me."

"Okay, but first, could I take a look at your bible?"

Confused, Alex responded, "Of course." He proceeded to take his bible out of the desk drawer and handed it to Rick.

Thumbing through it, Rick said, "I have to admit, I don't know much about the bible. Could you help me find the book of Isaiah?"

Alex walked around the desk and helped him find it.

When he found chapter seven, verse fourteen, he read aloud, "Therefore the Lord himself will give you a sign: The virgin will be with child and will give birth to a son, and will call him Emmanuel."

Pastor Alex noticed that Rick's face had gone white. He asked, "Are you okay?"

"What does that passage mean?"

"It's a prophecy. It foretold the birth of Christ."

"What about the name 'Emmanuel?'"

"In the Hebrew language, it means 'God with us.'"

"So Emmanuel and Jesus are one and the same?"

"Yes. Jesus was God, who came to the earth in the flesh. He was in fact, God with us."

Rick stood up and looked out the window. "You'll probably find this hard to believe, but I think that I just met Jesus."

"What makes you say that?"

Rick sat back down and began telling the pastor everything that had happened after his attorney dropped him off at Floyd's Pub. When he finished, they both stayed silent for a few seconds.

Alex asked him, "He told you that his name is Emmanuel?"

Rick nodded slowly. "I don't know how he knew so much about me. I was irritated by him at first, but as he talked to me, I felt a calmness that I've never felt before. It was odd. I feel like I can trust him."

"Could you describe him for me?"

"Shoulder length brown hair and a beard. Tall and thin. He wasn't dressed like you would expect him to be. You know, the way that he's depicted in movies. He had a gray hoodie and jeans. White shoes, too, if I remember correctly."

Pastor Alex leaned back in his chair. Could this be the same man that Matthew Peters and his friends had encountered? He thought about the man that he'd seen while sitting at the red light the other day. Rick's description matched perfectly. Alex was pretty sure that they were the same guy.

He knew that he had to tread lightly. Rick was obviously at a crossroad and saying the wrong thing could send him back to his destructive ways.

Before he had the chance to say anything, Rick said, "I don't know much about God or Jesus, but I'd like to learn."

Alex smiled as he felt the adrenaline start to pump through his veins. "The most important decision that you'll make in your life is whether or not you'll accept Jesus Christ as your Lord and Savior. It's a decision that has eternal consequences."

"Eternal? How's that?"

"That decision dictates where you're going to spend eternity after you die. Heaven or hell. The choice is up to you."

Rick leaned forward with a confused look on his face. "Getting into heaven is as simple as asking Jesus into my life?"

"It's the only way. John 14:6 says, 'I am the way and the truth and the life. No one comes to the Father except through me.' You see, Rick, Jesus came to earth to die for all of our sins. Mine, yours, and everyone else's. All we have to do is acknowledge that, accept him into our lives, and ask him to forgive our sins."

"You make it sound so simple."

"It is. People try to make it so complicated, but it's very cut and dry."

Rick ran his fingers through his hair and sighed. "What about just trying to live a good life?"

"Who's standard of good are you talking about? Yours or God's?"

Rick looked perplexed. "What's the difference?"

"None of us can live up to God's standard. That's why he sent his Son to die on the cross for us. He paid the penalty so we wouldn't have to."

"That's very sobering."

"Going back to what you said about living a good life, that's a common misconception. Nowhere in the bible does it say that good people go to heaven and bad people go to hell. I'm not sure where that came from, but it's not biblical. The bible is very clear that the only way to heaven is to accept Jesus as your Lord and Savior and ask for His forgiveness."

"Well, that sounds great for when you're dead, but what about now? How can becoming a Christian help me with what I'm going through?"

"Never underestimate the power of prayer. The most important thing for you right now is to stop drinking. When you're struggling and being tempted to take another drink, you can pray. Hebrews 2:18 promises that He will come to our aid whenever we are tempted. We just have to ask for it."

"What if I give in to temptation?"

"We all fall from time to time. When it happens, recognize it and ask God to forgive you."

"Is getting forgiveness really that easy? I've done a lot of things that I'm not proud of. Hitting my son is just the beginning. How can God forgive someone like me?"

"Are you truly sorry for the things you've done?"

"Yes. I really am. While I was driving over here, I kept thinking about how I've been living my life since my wife died. Even before that, I was doing things behind her back that I shouldn't have been doing. I was a lousy husband, a terrible father, and I've spent my whole life being selfish. I don't want to be that man anymore."

Pastor Alex stood up and walked around his desk, crouched down next to Rick and asked, "Do you want to give your life to Christ?"

Rick began sobbing. "Yes."

Alex put his arm around Rick's shoulder and whispered in his ear, "Ask him into your life."

Rick slowly dropped to his knees and stared praying, "God. Jesus. I'm not proud of the way I've lived my life. Please come into my heart and change me from the inside out. Help me to become a better man. I realize now, that doing things my way doesn't work. I want to try things your way. Please forgive me for hitting my son. Please forgive me for abusing my body with alcohol. Please forgive me for being a horrible father. Please help me with my alcohol addiction. I never want to take another drink again, but I know that I can't do it by myself. Please give me the strength to say no when the temptation arises. Most of all, Jesus, I want to thank you for paying the price for my sins. Forgive me and come into my life. Amen."

Rick opened his eyes and saw Pastor Alex smiling down at him. "Welcome to the family. We're brothers in Christ now."

Getting back to his feet, Rick said, "My heart was beating so fast. I feel better now than I've ever felt from drinking."

"There's no high like the Most High."

"Huh?"

Alex laughed and said, "Never mind. The important thing is that now you're a Christian."

"What do I do now?"

"I would recommend that you start attending church. It doesn't have to be here, but you're always welcome. Go to meetings to help your alcohol addiction. Get involved with some bible study groups."

"This is hard for me to get a grip on. It's all new to me."

Alex went over to a shelf against the wall and pulled down a bible. "I want you to have this. Read it in your spare time. I suggest that you start with the Gospel of John. Learn about Jesus. You'll be amazed with what you read in here."

Rick took a deep breath. "I'll do that, but I'm scared. The thought of never drinking again is overwhelming."

"Don't rely on your own strength. Rely on God's strength."

He nodded and said, "I'd like to talk to my son. Do you have the number for where he's staying?"

Alex looked through the church directory and found the number. He wrote it down and handed it to Rick. "You can call him here. I'll step out and give you some privacy."

He left the office and closed the door behind him.

Fifteen minutes later, Rick emerged from the office looking like a new man. They shook hands and Alex wished him well. As Rick left the parking lot, Alex watched him leave with a big smile on his face. This was one of the moments that made being a pastor worthwhile.

CHAPTER 20

Matthew and John sat next to each other on the school bus. They were returning from the JV game, where they had just finished another convincing victory. Matthew had a spectacular game, throwing three touchdown passes. John played well, too, scoring his first career touchdown on an interception return.

Despite the win, John sat staring out the window, not saying a word. Matthew tried talking to him a few times, but John was clearly distracted and shrugged him off each time.

Finally, Matthew asked, "What's bothering you? And don't tell me that it's nothing. I know you too well for that."

John sighed and said, "I'm thinking about Tim. He's leaving for Philly tomorrow morning. This has got to be tough for him. He's going to have to start all over at a new school. With everything that he's been through, a new school will be a really hard adjustment for him."

"Kylie is handling being a new student pretty well."

"Sure, but Kylie is pretty and outgoing. Tim is kind of shy and laid back. He'll have a much harder time making friends."

Matthew thought about that for a few seconds before agreeing. "You're right. Maybe we should pray for him."

"Right now?"

"Why not?"

John looked over his shoulder at the rest of the team. "Won't that be awkward in front of everyone?"

"So what? They probably won't even know what we're doing."

"Okay." John looked uncomfortable as he closed his eyes and started praying. "Lord God, we want to thank You for everything that You've been doing in our lives. Thank You for sending Emmanuel to us, and thank You for the great advice He's given us. We want to lift our friend, Tim, up to You. You know what has happened recently and the circumstances that have led up to this. We just ask that You be with him. Guide and protect him. Help him to find good Christian friends at his new school. Help him to adjust well. We also want to lift his grandparents up to You. Help them to make the right decisions in his difficult situation. Keep them all safe and allow Your will to be done in their lives. All of this in Jesus' name we pray. Amen."

Matthew repeated, "Amen."

John opened his eyes and looked around. To his surprise, nobody was even looking at him. He had expected everyone to be staring at him. He even feared that they would ridicule him. He breathed a sigh of relief and looked at Matthew with a smile. "Thanks. I feel a little better now."

Matthew chuckled and nudged him with his elbow. "Don't be getting all sappy on me."

John laughed and said, "I don't think so!" He put Matthew in a headlock with his left arm and rubbed his right knuckles against his scalp. "You might be the star quarterback, but I can still whoop your butt."

They wrestled around in the seat until an assistant coach yelled from the front of the bus for them to stop. They laughed hysterically for a good minute. When they regained their composure, John asked him, "Is there anything going on between you and Kylie?"

"Not yet. I'm following Emmanuel's advice and being friends first. It's not easy sometimes. I think that she's the most beautiful girl I've ever met."

"Now who's getting sappy? That's cool though. Just give it some time. It's obvious that she likes you, too."

"Really?"

"You would have to be blind not to see it."

Matthew was grinning from ear to ear. "I hope you're right. What about you? You and Madison talked quite a bit the other night at Mario's."

John turned around to see if Mark was listening. When he saw him joking around with some of the other players a few rows back, he said, "I'm not sure what to make of it. I'm attracted to her, and we get along really well, but it might be weird dating Mark's sister. Not to mention the fact that she's two years older than me."

"Do you think that Mark would have a problem with it?"

"I don't know. He's a tough one to figure out sometimes."

"I'll talk to him for you, if you want."

"No. Not yet. I haven't even made my decision yet. If I decide to pursue her, then I'll worry about it."

The bus pulled into the school parking lot. As soon as John exited the bus, he saw Pops and Tim standing next to the minivan, waiting to give them a ride home. He waved to them as he headed to the locker room to put his equipment away.

—

Matthew was thinking about all that was happening in his life. Despite the rocky start, he was thrilled with how his freshman year had gone so far.

As he was about to go back outside, Coach King called for him to come back to his office. Matthew suddenly got nervous. He entered the office and sheepishly asked, "What's up, Coach?"

"You played an awesome game today, and you played an amazing game Friday night. With that said, I need to tell you that I'm going to start Cody at quarterback this week. It's not because you played badly. You know better than that. I know that Cody hasn't looked good in the last two games, but I'm going to work very close with him this week, and I think that with a little help, he'll be ready."

Matthew's adrenaline rush from the JV win suddenly evaporated. He exhaled deeply as disappointment settled in. "This wouldn't have anything to do with the pressure Cody's dad is putting on you, would it?"

Coach King's eyes narrowed. "What do you mean?"

Matthew's face turned red with anger. "I saw you two arguing after the game, and then again in the church parking lot yesterday. I'm not an idiot, so don't treat me like one."

"You'd better lose that attitude, right now! You have no idea what you're talking about. As the head coach of this football team, I have a lot of difficult decisions to make, and I've made my decision about this. As for what Cody's father and I were discussing, that's none of your business and I don't want to hear another word about it."

Matthew turned around and stormed out of the office. He was so livid that he was practically stomping his feet as he walked to the minivan.

When he got inside, Luke asked, "What are you so mad about?"

"I just talked to the coach. I'm still second string."

Mark asked, "Are you kidding me? Doesn't the coach want to win?"

"You know what this is about. Cody's dad is on the school board and used his power to influence the coach."

Pops interjected, "You don't know that for sure. He's your coach and you have to respect his decisions. You're going to learn as you get older that this type of thing happens all the time in the real world. You'd better get used to it now."

Matthew kept silent. He knew better than to argue with Pops. He bit his tongue and remained silent the rest of the way home.

—

When they got back to the neighborhood, John asked Pops not to take him home. He wanted to spend some time with Tim before he went to Philadelphia. Matthew and Mark agreed to stay, too, so they all got out of the minivan in Luke's driveway.

They went around to the back of the house, where Pops had some patio furniture set up. As they took seats around the table, Pops came out with a pitcher of iced tea and five glasses, then returned inside to give the kids some privacy.

While Luke poured the iced tea into the glasses, John asked Tim, "Are you okay?"

"Actually, I am. I talked to my dad on the phone after school today. He had his hearing this morning. He pleaded guilty to a lesser charge and was sentenced to a year of probation. He told me that he's done drinking. He's going to start a twelve step program, but the best part is, he called the church when he was released and had a meeting with the pastor. He made the decision to give his life to Christ, right there in the church office. Apparently, Pastor Alex made quite an impression on him. He's going to be attending your church now."

John's eyes lit up. "That's awesome."

"I know that my mother is looking down from heaven with a huge smile on her face." Tears filled Tim's eyes, but they were tears of joy.

Luke said, "That's great news. Does Pops know?"

"Yeah. He was sitting right next to me when I talked to him. He was thrilled."

"I'll bet."

They were all smiling as they sat around the table, sipping iced tea. Tim continued, "I'm really proud of my dad. He has a long way to go, but he's on the right track. He sounded sincere when I talked to him. He really wants to get his life in order."

He stopped to think for a second before going on. "Do you know what's weird? When I woke up this morning, the pain in my ribs was almost completely gone. The doctor told me that they'd be sore for at least a few weeks. They're still a little tender, but nowhere near as bad as they were."

The others looked at each other. It was apparent that they were all thinking the same thing. Emmanuel must have had something to do with it.

John asked, "Have you seen your grandparents yet?"

"Yeah. They came over right after my dad called. I told them about our conversation. I thought that they would be happy about it, but they were skeptical. I guess that's to be expected. They still blame him for my mother's death."

"Where are they now?"

"They're staying at a hotel. They'll come get me in the morning and we'll hit the road. I'll start my new school Wednesday morning."

Mark smiled as he said, "I'll bet their football team needs a good kicker."

Tim almost jumped out of his seat as he exclaimed, "No! They have a soccer team. My grandfather knows the coach and talked to him. Even though the season has already started, they're going to let me join the team anyway. I'll be playing soccer again."

John reached across the table to give him a high five. He was thrilled for him.

They continued to talk for another forty-five minutes or so, before John said, "I'd better get home soon. I have a test tomorrow that I have to study for."

Matthew, Mark and Luke shook hands with Tim and wished him well. After they left to go inside, John gave Tim a long hug.

Tim said, "Thanks for everything. You and your friends made this much easier for me."

"You're welcome. You have my number and my email address. Keep in touch."

"I will."

"That soccer team is lucky to be getting you."

Tim blushed and turned to go inside.

John walked around the side of the house to go home. As he went down Forest Street, a single tear ran down his face. He was going to miss Tim, but he was no longer worried about him. He knew that God was looking after him and that he was going to land on his feet. He knew in his heart that Tim was going to be okay.

CHAPTER 21

Late Wednesday afternoon, Matthew and John waited outside the locker room for Mark and Luke to finish changing after football practice.

Matthew was still bitter about Coach King's decision to keep him as second string quarterback. Cody was showing no sign of improvement during practice, prompting Matthew to believe that the team had a much better chance of winning if he started. The thought frustrated him.

David encouraged him to be patient when they discussed it the night before. He was still a freshman and had a long high school career ahead of him. He reminded Matthew that he didn't start until his sophomore year, and that it was very rare for any school to have a freshman start at quarterback.

Matthew understood all that, but he wanted the team to win and didn't think that Cody had what it took to be a winning quarterback. He was happy that the JV team was undefeated, but he wanted the varsity team to do well, too. After losing two of the first three games, they would probably have to run the table if they wanted to make the state playoffs.

The next game was an away game against Penn Park, a traditional powerhouse team that competed for the conference championship virtually every year. Matthew knew that it would be a tough game and was itching to play. He wished the coach would come to his senses and let him start.

Mark and Luke came out and they began their walk home. As they turned onto Main Street, Emmanuel was standing there. Matthew saw him first and ran up to give him a hug. The others followed suit.

Emmanuel said, "I've been waiting for you. I have some things I'd like to discuss with all of you."

They started walking, eager to hear what he had to say. John spoke up first. "A lot has happened since the last time we saw you."

"I know. I was watching the whole time." He stopped walking and put his hand on John's shoulder. "You did a great job helping Tim. I'm proud of you. You can rest easy about him. He's already adjusting well to his new school. He's very happy to be on the soccer field again. His grandparents will take good care of him."

"I'm thinking about calling him tonight."

"I'm sure he would love to hear from you."

They continued walking and John said, "I'm confused about something. After the game Friday night, we saw how drunk Tim's dad was and prayed for him, but he got hurt anyway. Why did he get hurt after we prayed for him not to? Didn't God hear our prayer?"

"Of course He heard your prayer. He hears all of your prayers, but did you ever consider that it could have been a lot worse if you hadn't prayed?"

John looked up into Emmanuel's eyes and asked, "Would it have been?"

"Only my Father knows for sure, but I know that His will is being done through all of this. Have you ever heard the story from Exodus about how Moses freed the Israelites from Egyptian slavery?"

"Sure. What about it?"

"A lot of people get confused as to why God repeatedly hardened Pharaoh's heart. They wonder why God didn't just have Pharaoh release the Jews with the first request."

"I remember wondering about that when I first heard the story."

"First of all, the Israeli slaves needed to know that Moses really was sent by God. That's why the plagues were sent. They needed to see God's awesome power for themselves. They also needed to see their first born sons spared during the first Passover. Without these things, they never would have believed."

John looked astounded. "So, if God hadn't hardened Pharaoh's heart, they would never have had the faith to follow Moses to the promised land."

"Exactly, but there's more. As a result of Egypt getting hit with plague after plague, and then having all of their first born sons die, Pharaoh was eager to get rid of them. He even sent them away with a bunch of gold and treasure. This was the same gold that was used to make the Ark of the Covenant."

"So, all of those things that initially seemed bad were all a part of a bigger plan to complete God's will."

Emmanuel nodded and said, "Just like with your friend, Tim. He had to get beat bad enough to cry out for help. That led to his father's arrest. If that hadn't happened, his father never would have been broken enough to accept help from your pastor, and he never would have become a Christian. God knew what He was doing all along."

John shook his head in amazement. "It's so easy to overlook something like that. I guess I need to trust God in all areas of my life."

"Yes, you do. That goes for all of you." He turned to Luke who had been walking on his other side. "I want you to tell your grandfather to start eating healthier."

"Why?"

"If he doesn't, he's going to have health problems."

Luke pondered this for a few seconds, then said, "I have noticed a lot more junk food in the pantry. He's been gaining weight, too."

"Encourage him. He loves you and will be open to your advice."

Luke nodded and said, "I'll do that. I don't know what I'd do without Pops in my life."

Emmanuel then directed his attention to Matthew. "I see that you're angry with your coach."

"I'm frustrated. I know that I'm the better quarterback. The only reason that Cody is starting is because of the pressure his dad is putting on the coach. It's not fair."

"Whatever the reason may be, you have to respect his decision. Hebrews 13:17 says, 'Obey your leaders and submit to their authority.' Your coach is one of your leaders. If you respect his authority and not be bitter about his decision, God will honor that."

Matthew shook his head and said, "It's hard."

"You know that anger is a sin, right?"

"How can I not be angry? The position that I deserve has been given to someone else."

"You're being selfish. The football team is not all about you."

"I want to win. Not just for me, but for the whole team. How is that being selfish?"

Emmanuel looked him in the eye. "If Cody plays the entire game and your team wins, will that make you happy?"

Matthew thought about it and said, "No. You're right. I would rather play and lose than sit on the bench and win."

"That's something you need to work on. Keep working hard in practice, so that if the coach changes his mind, you'll be ready."

"Am I going to play this Friday?"

"Just be ready."

Emmanuel then asked Mark, "Are you still praying for Jude?"

"I have been. I still don't like him or his friends, but I'm trying to get past that. I sometimes think that praying for him is a lost cause."

"Prayer is never a lost cause. I already told you that my Father hears all of your prayers and takes them very seriously."

"I get nervous every time I'm out on the street like this. I never know when I'll see them again. I don't want to get beat like that again."

Emmanuel smiled and said, "I don't want that either. Those guys need help. Their souls are lost. Pray for people to be put in their path that will help them find their way."

John quickly nudged Emmanuel and said, "It looks like we're about to be put into their path." He pointed down the street.

About a block away, Jude, Scott and Ethan were walking toward them on the opposite side of the street.

Mark's face went white as he said, "We've got to get out of here!"

Emmanuel said, "Stay calm. I won't let anything happen. I want you all to stand here, side by side."

They did as Emmanuel said, standing next to each other, facing the street. Emmanuel stood between them and the street, facing the kids. He stretched his arms to his sides, parallel to the ground and looked to the sky. He said to them, "Stand perfectly still and don't say a word."

Mark said in a panic stricken voice, "They're going to see us."

"You need to trust me. When I said that I won't let anything happen to you, I meant it. Now, stay quiet until they pass by."

They were all uneasy, but didn't say anything else. Jude, Scott and Ethan walked by on the opposite side of the street and never looked their way. It was as though they were invisible to them. A few minutes went by and they were out of sight.

Mark breathed a sigh of relief and asked, "What just happened here? Why didn't they see us?"

Emmanuel laughed and said, "I told you that you could trust me."

Laughter ensued as they made their way home. Emmanuel walked a step behind them, joking around with the kids as they went. Having a great time, they enjoyed the time spent with him. They all felt like they had been friends with him forever.

John turned around to ask him a question and saw that he was gone. "Where did Emmanuel go?"

They all looked around with blank looks on their faces. Matthew said, "He was here a second ago. He must have pulled another disappearing act on us."

Luke laughed and said, "We shouldn't be surprised. He's done this before."

Mark had a serious look on his face when he asked, "Do you think we're the only ones he appears to?"

John said, "I've wondered that quite a bit myself. It does seem odd that of all the people in the world, he chooses to visit us. What makes us so special?"

Matthew said, "We're not special. He has no favorites. He loves us all equally."

John retorted, "If that's true, then why does he appear only to us? That sounds like favoritism to me."

"The next time we see him, we'll have to ask."

They walked the rest of the way home in silence.

CHAPTER 22

The team bus pulled into the Penn Park High School parking lot. Matthew exited the bus with his teammates and went into the visitors' locker room. He quietly put his uniform on and then went to the field to warm up.

Coach King was working with the first team offense. Matthew watched as Cody threw a few passes, some on target, and others way off the mark. It was obvious to anyone watching that Cody didn't have confidence in his own ability. The rest of the team had already lost their patience with him and it showed. Matthew thought to himself that it could be a long night.

The coach called the team back into the locker room for a last minute pep talk. He warned the defense to be on top of their game. The Penn Park Dragons had one of the best running backs in the state, a senior named Bryce Jacoby. He had rushed for over one-hundred-fifty yards in each of the previous games and had a large offensive line blocking for him. Coach King insisted that the top priority of the game was to stop Bryce Jacoby.

After praying with his friends, Matthew sprinted onto the field with the rest of the team. As the others shouted and hollered, getting themselves fired up, Matthew went over to the bench and sat down. He leaned forward and covered his face with his hands. He had been feeling guilty since his verbal exchange with the coach earlier in the week. He kept remembering what Emmanuel had said about obeying your leaders and submitting to their authority. He didn't want to, but he knew that apologizing was the right thing to do.

He walked up to Coach King and said, "I'm sorry for the way I disrespected you the other day. You're my coach and I will abide by your decisions, whether I agree with them or not."

Coach King had been looking at his clipboard. He lowered it and said, "I appreciate you saying that. You're a smart kid, Matthew. You have a very bright future ahead of you. I want you to be ready, because if Cody plays the same way he has the last two weeks, you'll be getting another chance."

"I'll be ready."

Matthew went back to the bench and looked up into the bleachers. They were packed! He was surprised when he saw how many Benworth fans showed up. He expected a low turnout because Penn Park was about a forty-five minute drive, and the fact that they were on a two game losing streak. For whatever reason, the fans continued to support the team.

Despite the large number of fans, Matthew easily found Kylie, sitting with Jocelyn, Madison, and several other girls that she had made friends with over the last few weeks. She appeared to be having a great time, laughing and talking with them. He chuckled to himself. He couldn't believe how hard he was falling for her. He turned around to see the start of the game.

—

Penn Park won the toss and elected to receive. They took the field in their home uniforms, navy blue jerseys with gold numbers and pants.

Tim's departure from the team left an opening at the kicker position. Donavan Ward was a senior offensive lineman who had done some kicking on the JV team in previous years, so the kicking duties now fell on him. He was a large kid with a powerful leg. He could kick the ball farther than Tim, but wasn't nearly as accurate.

Donavan teed the ball and began the game by kicking the ball over the deep man's head and through the back of the end zone for a touchback. He returned to the sideline, receiving high fives and fist bumps from his teammates.

The defense, knowing that they were one of the best in the conference, lined up for the first play. All eleven players had one objective on their minds, stop Bryce Jacoby!

They didn't fare too well. The Dragons offensive line was overpowering the Eagles defense, creating big holes for Bryce to run through. He was picking up seven or eight yards almost every play. In addition to the great blocking he was getting, his speed and agility was proving to be too much for the Benworth defense. On the tenth play of the drive, Penn Park had the ball on the Eagles eleven yard line. Once again, Bryce carried the ball, a sweep around the right side. He broke two tackles and leapt over another defender, who had tried to take his legs out from under him, on his way to the end zone. Five minutes into the game, the Eagles trailed 7-0, and Penn Park hadn't even thrown a pass yet.

The body language of the Benworth players seemed to say *Here we go again!* They got ready to receive the kickoff without any enthusiasm. Hunter returned the kick to the thirty yard line.

Cody slowly jogged onto the field. Rather than try to psych his players up, like a good team leader should, he went to the huddle with his shoulders slumped.

The drive started out pretty good, with Hunter gaining decent yardage on the first few plays. Cody even completed his first two passes to Dylan. They moved the ball deep into Penn Park territory before Cody ended the drive by throwing an interception into the end zone.

The Dragons second possession was just as successful as the first. They drove straight down the field, with Bryce carrying the bulk of the load. He scored his second touchdown of the night and Penn Park led 14-0 at the close of the first quarter.

Benworth got close enough to kick a field goal early in the second quarter, but on Penn Parks' next drive, they scored again to make it 21-3.

Cody's play got worse as the game went on. Halfway through the second quarter, he threw his second interception of the night. The Eagles defense stood strong this time, forcing the Dragons to punt, but once again, Cody threw another interception to bring an end to the first half.

—

The team returned to the locker room, looking dejected and defeated. Coach King separated the defensive starters from the rest of the team. The defensive coordinator took the defense to the side to discuss the adjustments that were desperately needed. Bryce Jacoby was making the defense look foolish and they had to change some things if they wanted any chance to win this game.

Before Coach King said anything to the team, he crossed the locker room to where Matthew was sitting, bent down, and whispered in his ear, "You're going to start the second half. Are you ready?"

"Of course." A combination of nervous energy and excitement coursed through his body.

The coach then walked over to Cody and whispered in his ear. Matthew couldn't hear what was said, but it didn't seem to phase Cody in any way. He sat looking straight ahead, with a blank look on his face, slouched on the bench with his arms folded. If he was angry about being benched, his demeanor didn't show it. He just sat there, staring off into space, not even acknowledging what the coach had told him.

Coach King went back to the front of the room to address his team. "Matthew will be playing quarterback for the rest of the game."

This seemed to liven the players up a little. Several shifted their bodies in their seats and listened intently to what their coach had to say. Little by little, Coach King's speech started to fire the team up. By the time they returned to the field, the majority of the players believed that they could still win this game.

The second half began with Hunter receiving the kickoff at the ten yard line. He followed his wall of blockers and made a cut to the left when he saw that he had a lot of running room to that side. He made his way up the left sideline and crossed midfield. He was pushed out of bounds at the Penn Park forty yard line.

The fans came to life and were cheering Hunter's kick return, and the cheering got even louder when they saw Matthew run out onto the field.

Matthew called the play and as the offense broke the huddle, he nudged Dylan and said, "Go deep!"

Dylan nodded and lined up as a wide out to the right side.

Matthew took the snap, faked a handoff to Hunter, and dropped back to pass. Dylan ran straight down the right side of the field, a step ahead of his defender. The free safety saw this and ran over to give support just as Matthew threw a long, high pass. Dylan continued to dash downfield, and as the ball came down, he leaped up at the same time as both defenders, at the five yard line. Due to his height advantage, he managed to jump a little higher than the Penn Park players, and came down with the ball. Both defensive players wrapped him up for the tackle, but his momentum carried them across the goal line.

Matthew pumped his fist back and forth, then dropped to his left knee and pointed his right index finger to the sky, imitating some of his favorite NFL players that he'd seen on TV, silently giving praise to God.

The excitement on the Benworth sideline was electric. Players were slapping each other on the back and shouting encouragement.

Donavan missed the extra point, but it didn't diminish their fervor.

After the kickoff, a pumped-up defense lined up. The new strategy was to completely forget about defending the pass. They knew that Penn Park would most likely play conservatively, trying to protect the lead. Three consecutive running plays were stuffed by the Benworth defense, and the Dragons punted the ball back to the Eagles.

The teams' confidence was soaring as Matthew led the offense back onto the field. They marched the ball downfield with a good mix of running plays and short passes, with Hunter looking just as good as Bryce. Matthew did a good job of throwing to different receivers, keeping the Penn Park defense off balance.

The drive took a lot of time off of the clock. With just over two minutes left in the third quarter, Hunter capped off the drive with a three yard touchdown run, cutting the deficit to 21-16.

There was a buzz going through the Benworth bleachers. They were excited and making a lot of noise.

The Penn Park side of the field had gone silent. Their fans had worried looks on their faces. The momentum of the game had shifted, and they weren't happy about it.

The Dragons' next possession had much more success. They used a good mix of their own to confuse the defense. They picked up a first down as the third quarter ended.

The fourth quarter started with Penn Park continuing to move the ball, picking up first downs and chewing up time on the clock. They managed to get inside the twenty yard line before the Benworth defense tightened up, forcing a field goal. The Dragons led 24-16 with 8:46 remaining.

The Penn Park kickoff coverage was excellent, keeping Hunter's return short. The Eagles started their drive at the sixteen yard line. Matthew did his best to keep the teams' morale up. When he got to the huddle, he said, "Come on, guys! We still have plenty of time. Just like the last drive, let's shove the ball right down their throats!"

The rest of the players showed their support with shouts of approval. Matthew was on fire, leading the team downfield with precise passes, picking apart the Dragons' defense. The only downside was that the receivers were staying inbounds, keeping the clock moving. The clock was becoming their enemy.

They got to the ten yard line, but an incomplete pass, followed by a sack, produced a fourth and long situation with 3:34 left in the game. Coach King opted for a field goal attempt, much to the dismay of the Benworth fans. Donavan made the kick, and the Eagles trailed 24-19.

Coach King gathered the defense together while the kicking team ran onto the field. "We have to stop them. We have all three timeouts remaining, but I don't want to use them on defense. Three and out. Don't let them get a first down."

Donavan once again put his powerful leg to use, kicking the ball deep for a touchback. The Dragons would start at the twenty yard line and no time came off of the clock.

The defense lined up, knowing that Bryce was likely to run the ball. Not surprisingly, Bryce carried the ball and was gang tackled after a one yard gain. Penn Park took their time calling the next play, while valuable time ticked off the clock.

Second down wasn't much different as Bryce picked up two yards. The defense was excited as they lined up for the third down play. Maybe a little too excited, because they over-pursued as Bryce ran a sweep to the left side. He cut back to the middle of the field, leaving the Benworth defense scrambling to keep up. He picked up ten yards and a first down, as the clock dipped below two minutes remaining.

Coach King took off his baseball cap and threw it to the ground in disgust. Now they would have to use their timeouts on defense to stop the clock. You could feel the life coming out of the Benworth side of the field.

Penn Park waited until the last possible second to snap the ball without getting a delay of game penalty. Bryce ran the ball for two yards and the Eagles quickly called their first timeout with 1:26 left. He was stopped for no gain on second down and another timeout. Third down was identical to the previous play and Benworth used its final timeout with 1:12 to go.

The punt was high and the coverage was good, forcing Hunter to call for a fair catch at the thirty-eight yard line. The punt took another ten seconds off of the clock. They were sixty-two yards from pay dirt and had just over a minute to get there.

Matthew called the offense together in the huddle and said, "Let's go, guys! We can do this!" He felt odd, trying to psych his players up. He couldn't believe that the seniors on this team would take a freshman seriously, for leadership. That concern evaporated fast, as he saw that the entire offense was hanging on every word he said. He continued, "Linemen, you've been doing a great job blocking all night. Just keep doing what you've been doing. Receivers, get open and I'll put the ball in your hands. Try to get out of bounds. We don't have any timeouts left. If you can't get out of bounds, line up as fast as you can, so I can spike the ball."

They went up to the line of scrimmage and fans on both sides of the field rose to their feet. Matthew took the snap and completed a screen pass to Hunter, who ran up the sideline and out of bounds at midfield.

Two more completions took them to the twenty-five yard line, but his receiver was tackled inbounds.

Matthew was screaming to his players to line up fast, as the clock kept ticking. He finally spiked the ball with twenty-four seconds left.

The next play, he hit Dylan for a six yard gain with a sideline pass. He casually stepped out of bounds with nineteen seconds on the clock.

When the players went back to the huddle, Matthew noticed how tired they looked. "Come on, guys! Suck it up!" His confidence was at an all time high. He knew that he could lead this team to victory. He scanned the players and his eyes locked with Dylan's. He saw a determined look on his face and knew right away that his next pass had to go Dylan's way. He said to him, "Run a post pattern. I'll get it to you."

Dylan gave him a firm nod and the team lined up. Matthew took the snap from the shotgun formation and dropped back. He threw the ball over the middle and Dylan was there to make the catch at the five yard line. The free safety ran up from his position at the goal line and dove for Dylan's ankles, taking his feet out from under him. He came down on the three yard line, but the clock was still moving.

Matthew ran up to the line, yelling out for everyone to line up. As soon as they were in position, he called for the snap and spiked the ball. He turned to look at the scoreboard and saw that the clock had stopped with three seconds remaining.

He breathed a sigh of relief and called the offense to the huddle. He looked to the sideline to get the signals from the coach. "Alright! Bootleg option to the right. Receivers, make sure that you're ready. The first open man I see, I'm going to rifle it to you."

The team was fired up as they approached the line of scrimmage. The defense was just as pumped up. Fans on both sides of the field were cheering as loud as they could. Everyone was on their feet.

Matthew barked out the signals and took the snap from under center. He faked a handoff to Hunter and rolled to his right. He looked for an open receiver, but they were all covered too well.

He was going to have to run it in himself!

He tucked the ball and lowered his shoulder. A Penn Park linebacker rushed up to meet him. Matthew wasn't sure if he could get to the end zone, so he dove head first. The linebacker grabbed him around the knees while he was in midair. Matthew felt his momentum stop, as he started to come down. Time seemed to stand still as he realized that he was going to fall short of the goal line.

In a desperate attempt, he reached out his arms as far as he could, trying to stretch the ball across the goal line. He came crashing to the ground with a thud! A second defensive player came down on top of him. He tried to see if the ball had broken the plane of the end zone, but he couldn't see.

The Penn Park players were waving their arms in front of them, signifying that he was stopped short, while the Benworth players had their arms above their heads, saying that it was a touchdown.

After what seemed like an eternity, the referee finally raised his arms to the sky. It was a touchdown!

While Matthew was still on the ground, sprawled out, the rest of the team began piling on top of him. The players ran onto the field from the bench, screaming and shouting. Many of the fans even jumped the fence to run onto the field, as well. They were all jumping up and down, sharing hugs and celebrating the victory as though it were the Super Bowl.

They didn't even bother kicking the extra point. The final score was 25-24.

When his teammates, who had piled on top of him, finally got up, Matthew got to his feet, took off his helmet, raised in in the air and shouted at the top of his lungs. His adrenaline was pumping harder than it ever had in his life. He felt like he was walking on air. It seemed like everyone was rushing over to congratulate him. It was overwhelming.

He managed to break free from the crowd and started heading back to the locker room, when he saw Kylie out of the corner of his eye. She had climbed the fence and was running straight for him. She wrapped her arms around his neck as he picked her up by the waist, twirling her around three times before setting her down.

"You were awesome!"

He blushed as she planted a kiss on his cheek. He said goodbye as he ran to the locker room. As he was about to enter, he saw Emmanuel standing off to the side. Emmanuel smiled at him, gave him a nod of approval, and turned to walk away, disappearing into the crowd.

Matthew laughed as he went into the locker room. He was feeling like he was on top of the world.

It got even better when Coach King came over to him and said, "Congratulations! You looked like your brother out there. Maybe even a little better!"

"Thanks, Coach."

"I want to tell you that you'll be starting from now on."

"Really?"

"You've earned it."

"What about Cody's dad?"

"You let me worry about him."

Matthew was smiling from ear to ear. The celebration continued the whole bus ride home. They were all in a jubilant mood, and they had a great time at Mario's Pizza.

It took a long time for Matthew to come down from his natural high. He was being treated like a celebrity, and he had to admit, he liked it.

Chapter 23

Matthew woke up the next morning and laid in bed, staring at the ceiling. He was wondering if the previous night was just a dream. It all seemed surreal.

When he tried to stand up, the soreness that engulfed his body from some of the hits that he received gave him confirmation that it was a reality. He really did lead his team to an amazing come from behind win. He smiled despite the pain.

He walked around the room, trying to loosen his muscles. Shaking the cobwebs out, he laughed to himself as he recalled the events of last night's game.

Grabbing his bible from the end table, he returned to his bed, propped up the pillows, got comfortable and began to read.

Earlier that week, he had asked Pops what his favorite bible story was, and he told him that it was the book of Daniel. Matthew figured that this was as good a day as any to learn about Daniel, so he started with chapter one and didn't stop reading until he was done with chapter six. He was thoroughly fascinated with the story.

He decided that he would read the remaining six chapters the next day. He got out of bed, showered, and ate a bowl of cereal for breakfast.

He flipped through some channels, trying to find something to watch, but couldn't find anything that caught his interest.

Thumbing through the latest issue of *Sports Illustrated* didn't help either, since he had already read it. He set the magazine down and sighed.

He was bored and itching for something to do. He was torn between calling the guys and spending a typical Saturday with them, or taking a chance and asking Kylie to go see a movie with him. Even though she turned him down the last time, he felt confident that she would say yes this time, due to the fact that they had grown much closer since then. He didn't want to rush things, but couldn't deny what he was feeling for her in his heart, either. He suddenly wished that Emmanuel was there to tell him what to do.

Wandering into the kitchen where his parents were having a quiet conversation at the table, he looked out the window into the backyard.

Emmanuel was sitting Indian style in the center of the lawn!

Matthew's eyes widened in surprise. He looked back at his parents, who didn't notice his look because they were just chatting amongst themselves. Looking back outside, they made eye contact, and Emmanuel motioned with his arm for Matthew to come outside and join him.

He held a finger up to let him know that he'd be right out. Returning to his room, he put on his shoes and slipped out back through the garage, so his parents wouldn't see him.

He greeted Emmanuel with a hug and asked, "What are you doing here? If my parents see me talking to you, they'll freak."

"They won't look out here."

"How do you know?"

Emmanuel just smiled at him. He asked, "How are you enjoying the book of Daniel?"

Matthew shook his head and said, "It sounds like you've been spying on me."

They both laughed, then Matthew got serious and said, "I do have a question about it. When Shadrach, Meshach and Abednego were put in the furnace, the king said that he saw four people walking around in the fire. Who was the fourth person?"

Emmanuel laughed again and asked, "You don't know?"

Looking confused, he said, "No." Suddenly, the realization hit him. "It was you?"

Emmanuel shrugged his shoulders and asked, "What do you think?"

"But … Daniel was from the Old Testament. You didn't even exist then."

"That's where you're wrong. I've always existed."

Matthew paced around the yard, letting that sink in. Smiling wide, he asked, "What did you think of the game last night?"

"You performed really well. Congratulations."

"I knew that if the coach gave me the chance, I could prove that I'm good enough to start. Now the coach agrees. He told me after the game that I'm the new starter."

"Are you sure you're ready for this?"

"I think I proved that last night."

Emmanuel frowned and said, "I'm glad that you decided to read the book of Daniel at this time."

Matthew thought about this for a few seconds, then sat down on the ground with his back leaning against the side of the house. Emmanuel sat facing him, a few yards away.

With an intent look on his face, Matthew said, "Something tells me that you may have had some influence on that."

Emmanuel scratched his beard and looked deep in thought. "Your newfound success on the football field is going to bring you popularity like you've never experienced before."

"I got a taste of that last night. I'll be honest, it felt pretty good."

"It's important that you don't let it go to your head. You're going to be learning leadership skills that are going to be valuable later in your life. Be careful to use them wisely. Just like with your brother, all of this can be taken away in a heartbeat."

Matthew gave him a stern look. "Speaking of that, why was it taken away from David? Although I'm very grateful to be the starting quarterback, I still feel bad for my brother. This was supposed to be his big year."

"Your brother reached a point where he felt like he didn't need God. He was totally relying on his own ability. My Father doesn't want that. He wants everyone to depend on him. Sometimes he takes things away so that they'll turn to him. Although he wasn't aware of it, your brother was heading down a road of destruction. My Father saved him from that life."

Matthew sat there, astonished. "I hope that doesn't happen to me."

"Stay close to me. You've been blessed with great athletic skill, but always remember that it came from my Father. Always give him thanks. He can take it away as fast as he gave it to you."

Matthew thought for a few seconds before responding, "I'd be devastated if I couldn't play ball anymore."

"I know that you love football, but there are a lot more important things in life. Keep your priorities straight."

"Is there anything else I can learn from Daniel?"

Emmanuel nodded enthusiastically, as if he were waiting for that question. "Just as Shadrach, Meshach and Abednego went into the furnace, your three friends are on the verge of going through fiery trials of their own. They're going to turn to you for support. They all look up to you.

As the leader of this group, you're going to need to be ready to help them through these tough times."

"The leader of the group? I've always thought of John as our leader."

Emmanuel nodded and said, "Up until now, he has been. Things are changing because of your achievements on the football field. Now, they're all going to start looking up to you, including John. You need to be ready for them."

Feeling a little surprised, he asked, "Will you be here to help me?"

"I'll always be with you."

Matthew looked to the sky and smiled for a few seconds, then looked back at Emmanuel. "You know, when I learned about you in Sunday school and read about you in the bible, I always pictured you to be so serious all the time. It was hard to imagine you with a sense of humor. Now that I'm getting to know you, I get the impression that you and your disciples probably had a lot of great times together. You could fit in with any group."

Emmanuel laughed out loud and said, "The three years that I spent with my disciples were so much fun. The gospels only scratch the surface of the things we did together. We had a lot of laughs and got to be great friends. It broke my heart to leave them behind when I ascended to my Father's side."

"Was your friendship with them similar to the relationship that I have with my friends?"

"In some ways, yes. In others, it wasn't. It was frustrating at times, but I wouldn't trade the time that I spent with them for anything. Cherish these friends that you have. They are a gift from my Father."

"What about Kylie? Will you give me the green light to date her?"

Emmanuel laughed again. "She's just as crazy about you as you are about her, but you need to be careful. Don't rush anything. You're both very young and a serious relationship is probably something that you should wait for. Just continue being her friend. She's not going anywhere."

Matthew was disappointed. "That's not the answer that I was looking for."

"I know, but you need to trust me. If you rush things, it'll end badly."

"I do trust you, but she's driving me crazy. How do I control myself?"

"Pray. Hebrews 2:18 promises that I'll come to your aid any time that you are being tempted. Ask for my help and I'll be there for you."

176

"I'll remember that."

Emmanuel rose to his feet and said, "I'd love to stay here and talk to you all day, but I have a lot of important things to do. I want you to remember something. With this new popularity that you're enjoying comes great responsibility. A lot of kids are going to look up to you. I want you to be a good role model for them."

"I'll do my best."

"You're emerging out from under your brother's shadow. Are you ready for that?"

Matthew climbed to his feet. "I think so."

"Any time that you need me, you can call on me. I may not always be here in the physical sense, like I am now, but I'm always with you. Do you understand?"

"I do."

Emmanuel hugged him and walked around the side of the house. Matthew watched him go. He thought about walking around the side of the house, but knew that if he did, he wouldn't see anyone. He knew that Emmanuel had gone on to other things.

He wondered if he would ever see him again. He desperately hoped that he would.

A sense of uneasiness covered him as he thought about the trials that his friends were about to face. Would he be able to help them the way Emmanuel expected?

He went back into the house with his mind racing. He had truly come out of the shadow, but was he ready for what the future held for him?